Nurse Alissa vs

the Zombies III

Firestorm

Nurse Alissa vs the Zombies III

Firestorm

Scott M. Baker

Also by Scott M. Baker

Novels
Nurse Alissa vs. the Zombies
Nurse Alissa vs. the Zombies: Escape
Shattered World I: Paris
Shattered World II: Russia
Shattered World III: China
The Vampire Hunters
Vampyrnomicon
Dominion
Rotter World
Rotter Nation
Rotter Apocalypse
Yeitso

Novellas
Nazi Ghouls From Space
Twilight of the Living Dead
This Is Why We Can't Have Nice Things During the Zombie Apocalypse

Anthologies
Cruise of the Living Dead and other Stories
Incident on Ironstone Lane and Other Horror Stories

A Schattenseite Book

Nurse Alissa vs. the Zombies III: Firestorm
by Scott M. Baker.
Copyright © 2020. All Rights Reserved.
ISBN: 978-1-7351312-3-8

To my fans.

Thank you for reading my books. You keep reading and I'll keep writing.

Chapter One

T HE SMALL TOWN the convoy entered seemed like so many others they had passed through during the last two months – either quiet and desolate, or overrun by the living dead. Those in the convoy would find out in a few minutes whether this town was clear or infested. Chances were fifty-fifty which, for Todd Dickson, were good odds. If a deader town, they'd plow right through. If vacant, they'd stop and replenish. The same procedures his team had followed since leaving Buffalo.

Nora Robbins watched the scenery pass from the passenger seat of their Hummer H3. "Where are we?"

"How the fuck do I know. What am I, a fucking GPS?"

"You don't have to be a dick about it," Nora huffed. She took the radio off the dashboard and keyed the microphone. "Jack, what town are we in?"

"*Waitsfield*," replied Jack Carter from the lead vehicle, a red Silverado 1500.

"Are we still in Vermont?"

"*As far as I can tell.*"

"Give me that." Dickson grabbed the radio, twisting it out of Nora's hand, and keyed the talk button. "What's the fucking deader situation like?"

"*Nothing so far.*"

"Good. If you see a good spot to pull over, do it."

"*Roger that, boss.*"

Dickson tossed the radio back on the dashboard.

Nora massaged her fingers. "That hurt."

"Don't be such a bitch."

"You know I hate it when you call me that."

"You're welcome to switch places with Diana if you want."

"That's okay." Nora lowered her head and focused her gaze out the window.

"I didn't think you would."

Nora had been more of a pain in the ass than an asset. They had picked her up a week or so after the clusterfuck in Henrietta when he needed new people, no matter who they were. He didn't expect much from her at first. She was only five feet two inches, in her early twenties, and a bit of a princess. Though not unattractive, she had that rough appearance of someone who has lived a hard life. She caught on quickly, learning how to use a firearm and a bladed weapon, how to effectively take down a deader, and how to be cold and hard to survive. Still, Nora remained the least capable of the team and constantly mouthed off, but she would do until someone better came along.

As the convoy entered town, it passed by the usual: residences, a florist, a cable company, an elementary school. But no humans or deaders. They hadn't come across anyone in several weeks. The living had either been eaten, become deaders, or, most likely, gone into hiding, which sucked. His team could always use more people. He couldn't blame them, though. The deaders were fucking horrendous to deal with. They had learned that the hard way outside of Rochester.

Dickson tried to repress those memories, which was futile. He'd never forget their attempt to escape the nightmare that engulfed Buffalo. Sure, they had planned on taking advantage of the situation. Why not? No one had ever given a shit about them, so now they looked out for themselves. But first, they had to make it to safety. Dickson thought he'd been smart by avoiding Rochester, the next big city east of Buffalo. However, not smart enough. He had chosen a major road that passed south through Henrietta, the bed and breakfast community for the city, and a location swarming with deaders. Twenty of them entered Henrietta. Four came out. Deaders got the rest: eleven friends, his two brothers and sister, his mother, and his fiancée. He would never forget their screams as the living dead tore them apart and devoured them alive. The arrogance of the two cops who drove by and didn't bother to help. And that fucking bastard who stole the Jeep from his younger brother, making his own escape and leaving Tommy behind to die. Since then he had played it safe, staying on back roads, avoiding cities and large towns, and always planning for the worst.

The lessons had been learned—the hard way. Their numbers had fluctuated since Henrietta, never coming close to matching the original twenty. Only himself and his best friend Stratman remained from the original group. They had survived and would eventually find a good place to settle down, somewhere isolated, defendable, and well stocked. Then he could concentrate on building up their ranks and making sure that, whenever this fucking apocalypse ended, he'd be in a position where no one would be able to push him around again.

The Silverado pulled off the road and into the parking lot of the Mad River Valley Ambulance Service. Dickson chuckled to himself. Damn, how appropriate.

Dickson pulled up alongside the Silverado. Carter climbed out of the pick-up. A burly guy, he stood six feet two inches in height and weighed close to two hundred and forty pounds, all of it muscle. With his curly red hair and beard, and the flannel shirt, Carter reminded Dickson of a lumberjack. Except a lumberjack didn't carry an AK-47 and wear a .357 Magnum and a hunting knife on his belt.

From the passenger seat, Tom Williamson came around the front of the Silverado and joined Carter. Dickson didn't want to bring Williamson along. The kid was a scrawny punk, not even twenty years old, who used to bully the other kids in high school, thinking that made him tough. They ran into Williamson hiding out in an abandoned truck stop in upstate New York. The kid gave them shit about how he owned the place and warned them to fuck off or else. The "or else" wound up being a fifteen-minute ass kicking by Carter. After that, the kid became more cooperative. Carter had taken a liking to him because the kid took his beating like a man, never once crying or begging Carter to stop. Afterwards, he asked that William-son be allowed to join the gang, and Dickson reluctantly agreed. Williamson wasn't tough, smart, or useful in any way, but he was pliable, and as such agreed to do a lot of the dirty work for Dickson, which made him handy to have around.

"Why'd we stop?"

Carter motioned toward the service center. "I saw three ambulances parked behind the building. I thought there might be something worthwhile in there. Besides, I need to take a leak."

"Do what you have to." Dickson nodded. "I'll get our little gophers."

He and Nora strolled across the parking lot as the last vehi-cles in the convoy pulled in—a black Mercedes-Benz Sprinter cargo van and an old, rusty, banged up 1999 Chevy 2500 pick-up truck with a decrepit cap covering the bed and a mis-matched right front fender still coated in primer. Elaine Vasco climbed out of the Sprinter. They had picked her up five weeks ago handcuffed in the back seat of an abandoned New York State Police car, malnourished, dehydrated, and wallowing in her own piss and shit. She had claimed the cops had arrested her for turning tricks to support her drug habit and then, in transit, left her when the deaders attacked. Dickson didn't buy it. Elaine did not act like a strung-out junkie. Besides, so many weeks into the apocalypse, the cops wouldn't be wasting their time on a street whore. It didn't matter. Elaine wanted to join, and he needed an extra body. They got her a shower, a new change of clothes, and nursed her back to health. Elaine waited by the van. She stood five feet six inches, now a little paunchy around the waist and face, with short dark hair and a face and body that wouldn't turn many heads.

Stratman leaned out the window of the pick-up. Six feet in height, Stratman sat crammed in behind the wheel of the Chevy. Clean shaven, close cut blonde hair, and sporting handsome features and piercing blue eyes, he had been a ladies' man in school, even with a few bitches who didn't want it. Not that Dickson cared. Stratman had always been loyal. They had been through a lot of tough times together and would see this one through as well.

"Everything okay?" Stratman asked.

"No problems. Carter found some ambulances he thinks might contain some useful supplies."

"Let me guess." Stratman opened the door and slid out onto the pavement. "You want the gophers."

"Just the asshole. We'll let the bitches and the kid get some air."

Elaine rushed over to the back of the pick-up. "Can I get him out? I still owe him for mouthing off to me last time."

Stratman tossed her the keys. Elaine unlocked the cap, raised the lid, and lowered the tailgate. She leaned over and smiled. Dickson could only describe it as malevolent.

"Morning, dickless." Reaching in, Elaine grasped onto something and dragged out a man in his thirties by his leg. She pulled him off the truck and let him fall. He hit the back of his head on the tailgate and landed hard on the pavement, moaning in pain. Elaine leaned over again and motioned with her hand. "Come on. You, too."

A woman in her thirties crawled out next, sliding along the tailgate and carefully lowering herself to the ground. Once out, she helped her two children, a young girl no more than nine and a boy almost fourteen. The woman went to help her husband, but Elaine pushed her back against the pick-up.

Reaching down, Elaine wrapped her right hand around the man's handcuffs and yanked him to his feet, ignoring his cry of pain.

"Stop whining. No one likes a snowflake."

"You could be more careful."

"Shut the fuck up, dickless." Elaine moved her hand as if about to punch the man.

"That's enough." Dickson walked up to them. Elaine backed off. Dickson removed the key, undid the man's handcuffs, and slid both into his pocket. "There are some ambulances behind the building. I need you to rummage through them for supplies."

"You promised to take care of us."

Dickson ignored him, not even bothering to face the man as he talked. "When you're done with the ambulances, check out the building itself and see if there's anything there we could use."

"My family hasn't eaten in days and we've not had anything to drink since yesterday morning. My family have peed themselves because you won't let us out to go to the bathroom."

"After that's taken care of, we'll stop for a short break."

The man said nothing. Dickson met his gaze. "Why aren't you moving?"

"I'm not going anywhere until my family gets—"

Dickson removed a Colt 1911 from his shoulder holster, placed the barrel against the man's face, and fired. The round ripped off the top of his head. His family gasped but did nothing, staring in shock at the upright body. It teetered a moment before collapsing, the wound gushing blood onto the pavement. The young girl held her older brother, averting her eyes away from the scene, wailing. The woman rushed forward and knelt by the body of her husband, caressing his chest and sobbing.

"No, Bobby. No."

Dickson reholstered the Colt. "Mrs. Taylor, I hope you were listening to the instructions I gave your husband. I don't like repeating myself."

"You didn't have to kill him, you fucking bastard!" she screamed, spittle and snot flying from her lips.

Dickson grabbed Diana by the ponytail, yanked her away from her husband, and slammed her against the side of the pick-up. Before she could respond, Dickson shoved his right knee between her legs, pushing them aside, and pressed his body against hers. He still clutched the ponytail. Leaning close, he whispered in her ear.

"You don't want a recurrence of your first night with us, do you?"

Her hands covered her groin and she mumbled, "No."

"And you don't want the same thing to happen to your daughter, do you?"

Diana shot her head up, her eyes pleading. "Please don't."

"Then what is it I need you to do?"

"Y-you need me to check the ambulances for supplies."

"And?"

Diana tried to think. Dickson yanked on her ponytail, causing her to gasp.

"And?"

"And you want me to check inside the building."

"Good girl." Dickson let go of the ponytail and lightly patted her cheek. He stepped away. Diana slid down the side of the pick-up and cried.

"Jim, go with her and provide cover."

"Why me?" protested Stratman. "I need to go take a shit."

"Fine, let Williamson do it."

Williamson moved up beside Diana and urged her to come with him. She had her head bowed, sobbing into her hand, and didn't see him. He reached down and gently touched her shoulder. Diana slapped his hand out of the way. Williamson grabbed her jacket and dragged her to her feet, ripping the fabric in the process. Shoving her in front of him, he placed his hand on her back and pushed.

"Hurry up, bitch."

The two children called out and went to follow their mother. Elaine placed herself in front of them. "You stay here and don't give me any trouble. Got it?"

The teenager hugged his younger sister and protected her, but backed off, leaning against the tailgate.

Dickson smiled. He'd let the others handle things for the next few hours. For now, he would grab some lunch and maybe take a nap before they hit the road again.

Chapter Two

14 February

What a wonderful surprise this morning! For Valentine's Day, Kiera and Little Stevie gave each of us hand-made cards. I knew they had been making them for their parents because they had been asking me for supplies for the past week. I hadn't expected to get one myself, and neither did Nathan. They also made one for Chris. We'll deliver his later today. When I asked Kiera why she and Little Stevie had given us one, she replied, "Because you're family now."

Steve's wounds are healing. He'll have reduced mobility for a while but, within a few weeks, will be up and about again. One good thing is that Steve, Miriam, and the kids have come closer together as a family. They play board games each night after dinner, Miriam reads to Little Stevie every day, and they both make the kids keep up with their learning, though it's difficult without textbooks. They seemed to have dealt with the trauma in their own way. It's so good to hear them laughing, joking, and having a good time.

Nathan and I have gotten a lot closer. We have late night talks, usually involving wine, where we reminisce about Nahant when we were kids and tell each other our life stories after graduation. If I had been this close to Nathan in high school who knows what would have happened.

Chris has become a regular visitor, which none of us mind. He's even spent a few nights sleeping on the couch. We all like

Chris. He's great with the kids and tells funny stories. Shithead is still terrified of Archer. I'm hoping after a bit they'll start to get along.

When I started writing this journal, I thought I'd be writing in it every day, recording daily adventures. The Chronicles of Apocalypse Alissa. It would have made a great movie. Instead, I experience brief moments of intense violence and terror that, afterwards, are too emotionally upsetting to put onto paper. The rest of the time we sit around battling boredom and cabin fever which, in their own way, can be as dangerous as a horde of deaders. My grandfather served as a marine during World War II. I remember him telling my father one night that he didn't know which was worse, the few days or weeks of combat when they stormed a Japanese-held island or the interminable months in between waiting for the nightmare to begin again. Now I understand what he meant.

Nathan has been doing a good job keeping us ready for what's coming next. Every day he trains us, including Chris, in the things he learned at the police academy: target practice, hand-to-hand combat, and how to strip and clean our weapons. Steve participates only in the firearm training. Nathan's not doing it to make us soldiers, which is never going to happen. He's doing it to make us confident and to keep us geared up for whenever we run into the living dead again.

The hardest part is dealing with the changes in our day-to-day lives. I know that sounds petty. People, families, entire generations are being eaten alive. Society across the globe has collapsed. Every individual has been impacted by this outbreak. Yet here I am whining about how the apocalypse disrupts my daily routine. What a pathetic bitch, right? But anyone who survives this crisis will understand what I mean. Sure, there have been natural disasters and pandemics that have disrupted the lives of millions of people before – Chernobyl, Hurricane Katrina, Ebola outbreaks in Africa, tsunamis in Thailand and Japan. Those were localized *events that had little impact throughout the rest of the world. Nothing on this scale has taken place since the flu pandemic of 1918 to 1920. It happened before. We should have realized it would happen again. We should have learned from the past and been prepared for something like this.*

We didn't.

We weren't.

Whenever a crisis struck another part of the world, we all watched in awe from the comfort of our homes and pitied those who were suffering. Never once did we think it could ever happen to us or, if that thought crossed our mind, we pushed it aside. We were too busy worrying about the present to plan for the future. Our daily routines revolved around trivial distractions. Sports, politics, video games, social media. Now that all those frivolities are gone, we're faced with an entirely different world none of us are ready for.

I used to come to this cabin to get away from it all and relax. Now I would kill for the commotion I tried to avoid. The isolation is disturbing. We are stuck here. No planes fly overhead. No cars pass by on the road at the foot of the mountain. No signs of civilization exist at all. It's too risky to go anywhere. We might get overwhelmed by a horde of deaders or, even worse, inadvertently lure them back here. Even if we did go out, where would we go? Nothing is open. No one is around.

Everyone here tries to cope with the isolation as best they can but it's slowly wearing away at our nerves. I spend as much time as possible exercising or sitting out here on the porch in the sun, reading or writing. The other day, a squirrel jumped up on the railing. I spent ten minutes feeding him bread from my sandwich. (If Archer had been sitting with me, things would have ended differently.) I had never spent the time to notice nature before. Now it's the most relaxing part of my day.

When this crisis is over and the world goes back to normal.... No, the world will never go back to what we consider "normal."

It's intriguing to imagine what society will be like when this has passed.

I thank God Paul had the foresight to realize what would happen and took the appropriate measures. Everyone in this cabin owes our lives to him.

The line between paranoia and preparation is razor thin.

"Alissa, are you ready?"

Kiera stood at the door to the porch.

"Ready for what?"

"Target practice."

"You're going?"

"Yes." Kiera beamed. "Uncle Nate said he'd show me how to use a gun."

"Then let's go." Alissa placed her pen between the open pages of her journal, closed it, and joined the others inside.

Kiera walked up to Nathan and Miriam. "We're ready."

"What do you mean 'we'?" Miriam asked.

"Uncle Nate is going to teach me to shoot."

Miriam shook her head. "I never approved that."

"I did," said Steve from the couch where he read a book. "She needs to learn how to defend herself if she's going to go on supply runs with you."

"She's not going on supply runs with us."

"I did last time."

"And you nearly got killed."

Using his finger to hold his place, Steve closed the book. "If I remember correctly, she saved your lives."

Kiera smiled the way only a teenager who had won an argument with her parents could.

Miriam stood her ground. "She won't be going with us again."

The smiled faded, "Why?"

"Because it's too dangerous. You'll stay behind and keep an eye on Stevie."

"I don't want to be a damn babysitter."

Miriam bristled. "Language, young lady."

Kiera looked to Alissa for support.

"We can discuss that later," said Steve, trying to broker a truce. "The fact remains that Kiera needs to know how to use a gun to defend herself."

"She's only fourteen."

"Don't worry," Nathan jumped in. "I used to train people who were going for their concealed weapon permits. I'll teach her gun safety and how to use one correctly."

"Does that mean I can carry one around like you do?" asked Kiera.

In unison, the four adults said, "No."

Kiera frowned.

"What about it?" asked Steve.

Miriam sighed. "I guess I have no choice."

Kiera pumped her fist.

Alissa leaned over and whispered in her ear. "Don't push your luck."

Gathering their weapons and some spare ammunition, Nathan led the way to the makeshift shooting range on the opposite side of the mountain.

THE MAKESHIFT SHOOTING range comprised nothing more than a wooden beam ten feet long and six feet off the ground, anchored on each end by two more wooden beams dug into the ground. Nathan had found an ideal location along the top of a ridge overlooking a gully. No trees were behind them for bullets to ricochet off. The gully was steep and wide enough that any deaders attracted by the gunfire would not be able to sneak up on them, nor could any humans approach without being seen or follow them back to the cabin without being detected.

As Alissa and Miriam stapled paper targets to the wooden beam and practiced shooting, Nathan stepped Kiera to the side and went over safety procedures with her.

"This is a Glock 23 semi-automatic pistol. It takes .40 caliber rounds. These are hollow point."

"What are hollow points?"

Nathan removed one from his pocket and handed it to Kiera. "A normal bullet is made of rounded metal for penetration effect. They will pass clean through a body and out the other side, leaving a small clear path. These collapse on impact, becoming a jagged metal disk that rips through the body. It's the difference between hitting a watermelon with a regular hammer and a sledgehammer."

Kiera handed back the bullet.

"I'm stressing this because an accidental discharge can be deadly to those around you, which brings me to the three rules you always have to follow when handling a weapon. If you forget these rules, I'll slap you on the head until you remember them."

"You wouldn't do that."

"If he doesn't, I will." Miriam flashed Kiera a disapproving glare and went back to practice shooting.

"Rule one. Never point the barrel at anything you don't want to shoot. Always keep the barrel pointed downrange. If you're carrying it in your hand in the field, keep it pointed at the ground. That way, if the weapon accidentally fires, you won't hurt anyone. Understood."

Kiera nodded.

"Rule two. When holding a firearm, always place your trigger finger on the frame, not the trigger guard." Nathan showed Kiera what he meant. "This way, when you're ready to fire, you have to make a conscious effort to move your finger to the trigger. If you rest it on the trigger guard, your finger could slip or you could unwittingly wrap it around the trigger."

Kiera positioned her fingers in the proper holding stance

and studied it for a second. "Gotcha."

"The third rule, and the most important one, is be aware of your surroundings. When you fire a round you are responsible for that round until it either hits something or falls harmlessly to the ground. This is extremely important in combat situations. If we're being attacked by deaders, and you must use your weapon, know what's beyond your target. If your mother or father, or Little Stevie, or anyone, is near your line of sight, don't pull the trigger. If your target moves, or you miss it, or if the bullet passes through, you could accidentally kill or wound one of us instead."

"What do I do in that situation?"

"Change your angle." Nathan aimed the Glock at a large pine tree off to their left. "What's behind that tree?"

"Other trees."

"Follow me." Nathan circled ninety degrees to his left, still citing the Glock on the tree. "Now what's behind that tree?"

"Open valley." Kiera's eyes widened. "I see what you mean."

"Now let's cover safety measures. When I first give you a weapon before we leave the cabin and upon our return, you must follow these procedures to ensure everyone's safety." Nathan went through the steps slowly, visually showing Kiera as he described the routine. "First, eject the magazine from the weapon."

Nathan popped out the fully loaded magazine and slid it into his back pocket.

"Pull the slide back until it locks open."

The round in the chamber flew out and fell to the dirt.

"Check inside and make certain there are no rounds in the barrel or the magazine chamber. Feel around inside with your pinky as a secondary check. Look away for a few seconds. Then visually check inside the weapon a second time. Where did I keep the gun trained when I did that?"

Kiera pointed in front of them. "That direction."

"It's called downrange."

"Downrange."

"Excellent." Nathan released the slide back into its normal position and showed her the next steps while verbally walking through them. "To load it, slide the magazine back in, and do it hard so it locks in place. Pull back on the slide and let it go. That loads a round in the chamber. Aim and fire."

A single bullet exited from the barrel, falling harmlessly into the gully. Holding the Glock by the grip with the barrel pointing downrange, he offered it to Kiera. "You try it."

Kiera reached for the weapon, pausing momentarily, not sure how to take it. She grasped the Glock by the barrel. Nathan released it. Kiera placed her left hand on the grip and transferred it to her right hand, her fingers away from the trigger. She followed the procedures Nathan had taught her, although taking much more time as she went through them in her mind. She performed each task perfectly, although somewhat awkwardly. When finished, she pointed the barrel at the ground and smiled.

"How did I do?"

"Excellent. I'm proud of you. Are you ready to shoot?"

"Fuck yeah."

"Kiera." Miriam had stopped firing long enough to flash her daughter the "mom look".

Nathan suppressed a grin and led her back to the shooting range. As Kiera stood at the firing line, he stepped forward and attached a target to the wooden beam and rejoined the others.

"To fire, hold the weapon in your right hand."

Kiera did, but with her forefinger resting on the trigger guard.

"Kiera!" Nathan barked.

She realized what she had done wrong and quickly placed her forefinger on the frame. "I'm sorry. I'm sorry."

"That's okay. Don't do it again."

"I won't."

"Now place your left hand on the weapon."

Kiera cupped the bottom of the grip in her left palm.

"Don't hold it that way. There's a good chance your left hand will push up, throwing off your aim." He removed Kiera's hand and placed it so her hand cupped the three fingers holding the grip. "You have better control this way. When firing, always keep your fingers on the frame and away from the barrel. That slide will tear up your finger. Raise the weapon so your right eye can see down the barrel but not too close. You don't want the slide recoiling into your face."

"You'll shoot your eye out," joked Alissa.

Nathan flashed her a stern expression then went back to training. "When the fluorescent dot on the front site is lined up with the two dots on the rear site, that's where your bullet will hit." Nathan stepped back. "Line up on the center of the target and fire a round."

Kiera took a good thirty seconds to line up the shot and fire. The recoil startled her. The bullet struck to the left and below center, barely hitting the silhouette.

"Try one more."

Kiera did, doing so in less time. The bullet struck close to the first one.

"I suck at this."

"No, you don't," Nathan reassured her. "You drop the gun to your left to compensate for the recoil. This time take a deep breath before firing, aim, and slowly exhale. Try to keep your gun steady. Fire two rounds."

Kiera did. The bullets struck within the black kill zone, missing the center by two inches.

"Awesome."

"Don't get cocky."

Each bullet drew closer, the last two hitting the center of the target.

"Bitchin'."

"Kiera," Miriam chastised her daughter again.

Nathan patted Kiera's shoulder. "You did a *bitchin'* job."

Miriam huffed.

"Reload and try again."

Kiera went through the procedure as Nathan had showed her, raised the Glock, and emptied the magazine. Five rounds hit the center of the target, four struck within the black kill zone, and the last four punctured the head.

"What happened?" asked Nathan. "The last three missed their target."

Kiera ejected the empty magazine, slid it in her back pocket, and checked the weapon for lodged rounds. "I aimed for the head. It's the only way to take down the deaders."

"Impressive."

"That's my girl." Miriam beamed with pride, having forgiven her daughter's earlier language.

"Hand me the Glock."

Kiera paused for a second. Nathan had not covered this. After a few seconds, she held the Glock by the bottom of the grip, the barrel pointing down, and passed it to Nathan.

"How'd I do?"

"Excellent."

"Better than me," added Alissa.

"First time gun users are usually better because they haven't developed the bad habits the rest of us have."

"And we play video games." Kiera turned to her mother. "See, all those hours playing *Doom* and *Resident Evil* paid off after all."

Miriam sighed.

"Can we do it again?" asked Kiera.

"Tomorrow. I don't want to waste too much ammunition."

Nathan rubbed Kiera's head. She rolled her eyes the way only a teenager could.

"Let's get back to the cabin," said Nathan.

CHRIS AND SHITHEAD were waiting for them when they returned, the latter curled up beside his master and keeping a close watch on Archer. As Miriam and Alissa made dinner and Nathan set the table, Kiera spent thirty minutes telling Chris and her father about her first shooting experience. Steve pretended to hang on her every word. Chris chatted with her about it, asking her questions and offering his own advice on gun safety and shooting. Since none of what he said contradicted what she had learned, Nathan didn't intervene.

After dinner, Miriam and the kids retired to the living room to play games while the others sat around the table chatting. Not about the outbreak, deaders, or the end of the world. They engaged in a normal conversation about books, movies, sports, and any other topic people normally talked about. It felt good, like a return to normal times.

Nathan had finished telling the others about *Seabiscuit*, the book he had read years ago about the famous racehorse, when Chris sat forward.

"That reminds me. You'll never guess what I saw a few days ago. A survivor riding a horse."

"Are you serious?" Stephen asked.

"I was on my front porch with my morning coffee when I saw him heading north along Route 302 toward Jericho."

"Did he seem..." Alissa searched for the correct word. "...friendly?"

"Hard to say. He had a backpack and saddle bag, and carried an AR-15, but other than that I couldn't tell."

"I hope you didn't attempt to get his attention?" asked Nathan.

Chris shook his head. "I watched him until he turned the bend and then waited fifteen minutes. He never came back."

"Good." Nathan sounded relieved.

"I wonder who he was and where he was going?" Alissa asked.

"I thought that as well," Chris responded. "He didn't seem frightened or in a hurry. Strange as it sounds, I found it comforting to know that we're not the last ones alive."

"He's probably wandering the countryside thinking the same thing." Stephen stood and limped into the kitchen. "The poor guy probably believes he's that last man on earth."

"I can assure you he isn't." Nathan grew solemn. "Most are in hiding, like us. The rest are the unlucky ones like your horseman who are stuck out in the open and those he definitely wants to avoid."

"Way to kill a good time," Alissa teased.

"I'm being honest."

"You're being paranoid. We're safe up here."

"For now." Nathan left the table and joined Stephen in the kitchen.

Chris waited until Nathan could not hear him and whispered to Alissa. "Don't be upset with Nathan. As a cop he's trained to go into every situation hoping for the best but expecting the worst."

"I wouldn't be alive if Nathan wasn't prepared to respond on a moment's notice, so I can't fault him when he gets this way."

"You're right about one thing," Chris offered in consolation.

"What's that?"

"It's a lot safer up here than it is out there on your own."

Chapter Three

JOEL EVANS RUMMAGED through the few remaining plastic bottles scattered across the floor, not finding anything of use. Body lotion, shampoo, underarm deodorant, toothpaste, hair dye, and a few gummy vitamins. Everything else had been stripped clean, especially the first aid section. Even the children's Band-Aids had all been scavenged, although in a way he was relieved. He didn't want to have to suffer the indignity of covering a major wound with a row of Band-Aids with images of Elsa and Olaf. Joel picked up the bottles of gummy vitamins and dropped them into his backpack. Who knows? Maybe they'll come in handy. Besides, it'll be a humorous story to one day tell his grandkids. If he lived that long.

When he and Rebecca stumbled across this pharmacy, neither expected to find enough supplies to last them several months, but they didn't expect it to be cleaned out. Everything that could be useful during the apocalypse had been cleared off the shelves. The only things left were the cosmetics and the Christmas cards and displays, and even the latter were down to only a few tacky items.

"What did you find?" asked Rebecca as she strolled down the aisle.

Even in dungarees and a utility shirt that were covered in weeks of dirt, and her unwashed blonde hair tied in a ponytail, she still looked beautiful. They had known each other since attending Dartmouth and had been dating for three months when the outbreak occurred. Since he lived in Chicago and had no way of returning home, she had invited him to stay with her parents at their farm in upstate New York. It had been perfect, if you didn't count that her parents had been taking a cruise in the Caribbean and had not been heard from since. They had become lovers and good friends. God knows what would have happened if a band of thugs hadn't wandered onto their compound one night three weeks ago, stolen the livestock, and ransacked the house. He and Rebecca barely made it out alive with their bug out bags and had been roaming the woods since. Their food and water had lasted less than a week, forcing them to resort to scavenging to stay alive, without much success.

"There's nothing except three bottles of gummy vitamins."

"Which type?"

"Multi-flavored."

"That's not what I meant." Rebecca knelt and lifted out each bottle. "Two Mickey Mouse and a Flintstones vitamin. Yabba dabba doomed."

"Really?"

"You have to maintain a sense of humor or you'll go insane."

"What did you find?"

Rebecca opened the bag and showed it to Joel. "Several pairs of pantyhose."

"What good are those?"

"They'll help keep you warm on a cold night."

"Hopefully, we won't have any more of those."

"We can help you with that."

Two men stood at the end of the aisle. Each carried an AK-47, the straps behind their necks, the weapons dangling in front of their chests. Rebecca reached under her winter coat and withdrew a Beretta 92FS 9mm pistol from its holster. The man on the left raised his AK-47 into firing position.

The other man stepped in front of his buddy and lifted his

hands in a gesture of surrender. "Calm down. We're not here to hurt you."

Rebecca did not lower the Beretta. "Then why are you here?"

"The same reason you are. We're gathering supplies."

"There's nothing left, so you can go." Rebecca tightened her grip on the trigger.

"I don't want any trouble." The man gestured for his friend to lower his weapon, which he did. "If I wanted to harm you, you'd both be dead by now. Besides, there are others outside. If you shoot us, they'll make sure you don't get out of here alive. Lower your gun."

Rebecca did nothing.

"Please."

Joel placed his hand on Rebecca's. "Put the gun away."

Rebecca lowered the weapon to her side.

The man stepped forward and offered his hand. "I'm Todd Dickson. The trigger-happy guy behind me is Jack Carter."

"I'm Joel." He shook Todd's hand. "This is Rebecca."

"A pleasure to meet you both." Todd went to shake Rebecca's hand but she declined. He shrugged and stepped back. "Did you find anything useful in here?"

"No," Rebecca answered curtly.

"I guess there's no need for us to check it out," Dickson said to Carter. He focused his attention back on Joel and Rebecca. "We've had the same problem. Every place has been stripped clean."

"I hear you," agreed Joel.

"Have you been on the road long?"

Rebecca answered for Joel. "Too long."

"Same here." Dickson allowed a short pause. "I can see you're both really low on supplies."

"We're fine," Rebecca insisted.

"You're not. I can see from here your backpacks are empty." Dickson remained pleasant. "We don't have much ourselves, but we can share some with you."

Joel's eyes widened. What luck. "That would be great. Th—"

Rebecca cut him off. "I said, we're fine."

Joel spun around to face Rebecca, his voice forceful but quiet. "Stop being rude. They want to help."

"They want something, but it's not to help."

"Excuse me," interrupted Dickson. "We'll wait outside while you talk this over."

"There's nothing to talk over," Rebecca responded.

"She's right," Joel snapped. "If you have something you can share with us, we'd appreciate that."

"Great." Dickson walked for the exit. "Follow me."

Rebecca grabbed Joel's arm and whispered. "Please, don't. I have a bad feeling about this."

Joel brushed her hand away. "Will you trust me? I know what I'm doing."

Joel stepped away and paused after several steps, waiting for his girlfriend. Rebecca stood still and glared at him, her eyes burning with fury. She lowered her gaze and followed Joel outside.

Four vehicles formed a U in the parking lot in front of the entrance: a black Hummer, two pick-up trucks, and a van. Two men and two women milled around the vehicles, none of them appearing to pose a threat. Joel didn't see any reason to be concerned, not even when he noticed a haggard young woman peering at him through the side window of the cap on the bed of the old pick-up truck mouthing the words. "Run. Run. Run."

"Elaine," Dickson called out. "Pop the trunk and give our friends some water."

The woman lifted the rear hatch of the Silverado. Joel leaned closer and peered inside. He spotted two twenty-packs of bottled spring water, one of them opened, an opened case of Spam, a dozen boxes of ammunition, and sundry other supplies. Dickson pulled out three bottles of water and strolled back to Joel and Rebecca, handing one to each of them. The third he kept for himself. Dickson twisted off the cap and tossed it onto the pavement, then raised his bottle in a toast.

"To survival."

Joel tapped his bottle against Dickson's and both men took a drink. Rebecca had not opened hers yet.

Joel finished half his bottle before stopping. "Damn, that's good. It's been a long time since I've had this much to drink."

"There's more where that came from."

"We couldn't take any more of your stuff. You need it."

"Don't worry about that." Dickson took another drink and smiled. "We're a team. We share everything with each other."

Alarm bells went off in Rebecca's mind. "We're not part of your team."

"You are now."

Only then did Joel realize what he had had gotten them into. "I appreciate the water. Rebecca and I prefer to be on our own."

"Nonsense." Dickson chuckled. "We all need to stick together if we hope to survive this."

"That's okay. But thanks for the offer."

"It's not an offer." Dickson still maintained an air of pleasantry although a menacing quality tinged his voice. "You're part of the team, whether you like it or not."

"Let's go," ordered Rebecca.

"Neither of you are going anywhere." Dickson glared at Rebecca with an intensity that caused her to avert her gaze.

Joel noticed that Carter and Elaine had unslung their weapons and were ready to use them at a moment's notice.

Dickson returned his attention to Joel. "Let's be reasonable. I'm surprised the two of you have lasted as long as you did on your own. Shit, we're finding it tough. If we combine our resources, we can better defend ourselves against deaders and we have more people to go into difficult places to gather supplies. You're part of the team. It's your choice if you join us or them."

Dickson pointed to the rear end of the Chevy pick-up. One of the other men had lifted the hatch and lowered the tailgate, revealing a woman and two kids in back, all of whom looked like they had gone through Hell.

"Who are they?" asked Joel.

"What's left of a family given the opportunity to join us and who opted out. We use the mother to scout out places so we don't run into deaders. The kids are insurance she does her job. So, what's it going to be? Are you with us or should I stick you in there with them?"

Shit, thought Joel. He should have listened to Rebecca. If they had left the store via the back exit, they might have had a chance. Now the two of them were trapped. Trying to sound as positive as possible, he responded. "We're with you."

"Good choice." Dickson gestured and the man closed the bed. "You two can ride with me and Nora in the Hummer. We have assault rifles that are much more effective in dealing with deaders than that Beretta your wife is carrying."

"Rebecca's my girlfriend."

"Perfect. Then you won't mind sharing her with us."

Joel stared at Dickson, dumbfounded. "What?"

"When I said we share everything, I meant it."

For a few seconds, Joel considered telling Dickson to fuck off and walking away, letting the cards fall where they may. Deep down he knew he didn't have that type of courage. He didn't want to die or, even worse, be shoved into the back of the pick-up and used as bait. Giving in was easier and safer.

Now if he could convince Rebecca of that.

Joel turned around to face Rebecca. "Honey?"

"Don't you call me honey, you spineless prick."

"I know this isn't easy—"

"Fuck off!"

Moving closer to Rebecca, he spoke softly so the others

couldn't here. "It's going to happen whether you agree or not. If you go along with them, we don't get shoved in the back of that pick-up."

"You don't get shoved in the back of that pick-up."

Her words hurt because they were true. "It's the only way."

"I bet you wouldn't be so willing to share if they wanted to shove their cocks up your ass." Rebecca sneered at him. "No, you'd suck them off if it meant staying alive."

"Please."

Rebecca slapped Joel so hard across the face it felt like he had been punched. She shoved Joel aside and confronted Dickson.

"Let's get this over with. I assume you're first?"

"Not me. My boys." Dickson glanced over his shoulder. "You guys can use the back of the van. And no rough stuff. Is that clear?"

"Yes," yelled Carter. He motioned for the other two men to follow. The three opened the back of the cargo van and ushered Rebecca inside. A minute later, the van began rocking.

Joel turned away so he didn't have to watch.

Dickson draped his left arm across Joel's shoulders and faced him back toward the van, talking to him like they were old friends. "I know it's tough at first, but you get used to it after a while. Besides, you can have your way with Nora and Elaine if you want. I meant it when I said we share everything. We cool?"

"Yes," Joel lied, wishing he did not have to keep his eyes on the van.

Dickson tapped his water bottle against Joel's and took a drink. "To survival."

After several minutes, the rocking stopped and the three men climbed out, straightening and zipping up their pants. They high fived each other.

Dickson nudged Joel forward. "Your turn."

"What do you mean?"

"Seal the deal. Once you've had your turn, you're part of the team."

Joel hesitated.

Dickson motioned with his head toward the van. "Go on."

Joel could not bring himself to see Rebecca like this.

"Do it." Dickson's harsh tone warned Joel this was his last chance.

Joel approached the van, bracing himself for what he would find. When he rounded the corner, his stomach churned. Rebecca's pants and underwear had been removed and her shirt and bra pushed up around her neck. They had not beaten or hurt Rebecca, only used her. She lay there, not even attempting to get up or get dressed. Her eyes stared at the ceiling, unmoving, as though, if she focused on one small portion of the van, she could forget about everything that had happened. The beautiful face that used to be so full of happiness and love now displayed only one emotion: humiliation. He had allowed the women he loved to be broken by his own cowardice. Dear God, what had he done?

Dickson cleared his throat loudly and pointed to inside the van.

Joel crawled in. Kneeling in front of Rebecca, he unbuckled his belt and lowered his trousers. As he drew nearer to Rebecca, her eyes turned to him. She scowled with a combination of pain, disgust, and fury. It nearly broke his heart. When he positioned himself on top of her, rather than except her lover passionately, she closed her eyes and turned her head to one side. Joel felt like a useless piece of shit.

Yet he did what he had to do to stay safe.

Chapter Four

T HE SUNLIGHT STREAMING through the bedroom window stirred Alissa awake. She rolled over, shading the rays with her hand. Her feet brushed Archer, who laid curled into a ball at the bottom of the bed, asleep. The cat stretched, one of those dramatic actions with the arched back and gaping jaw, then strolled up the mattress and cuddled up against her, purring loudly.

Alissa reached out and petted him. "Good morning, asshat."

Archer rubbed his head against her palm.

She checked the alarm clock. It read 9:17.

"I think we overslept."

Archer meowed, dived off the bed, and raced over to his food dish. His gaze alternated between his mistress and the empty bowl. When Alissa did not respond fast enough, he called the catastrophe to her attention with a prolonged meow.

"I love you, too."

Getting out of bed, Alissa opened one of the cans of wet cat food she kept on the bureau, emptied it into the dish, and cracked the window to dissipate the smell. As Archer gulped down his meal, Alissa freshened up, dressed, and headed downstairs, leaving the bedroom door ajar.

Only Little Stevie sat at the dining room table playing Nintendo Switch. He raised his head long enough to see who came downstairs before turning his attention back to the game.

"Hi, Aunt Alissa."

"Hello. What are you playing?"

"Animal Crossing. By the way, mom left your breakfast in the microwave."

"Thanks." Alissa passed by Little Stevie on her way to the kitchen, pausing to muss his air.

"Cooties," he said with a smile.

Alissa went into the kitchen and opened the microwave. Scrambled eggs and sausage. She would have to thank Miriam later for putting some aside. Punching one minute into the timer, she reheated the plate, pouring herself a cup of coffee while waiting. With her breakfast complete, she went back into the living area and sat at the dining room table across from Little Stevie.

"Where is everyone?" Alissa asked as she sipped her coffee.

"Nathan and Chris went out to sit on a parameter."

Alissa did a spit take onto the table. As she wiped up the mess with her napkin, she asked, "Do you mean set up a perimeter?"

Little Stevie shrugged. "I guess. They took Kiera with them."

"Where's your mom and dad."

Without taking his attention off the game, he rolled his eyes and pointed upstairs. Alissa listened. Through the floor, she heard the bed in the guest room squeaking. She suppressed a smile. Lucky them. Alissa could not remember the last time she had given her mattress a workout. Her mind went back to Nathan and Chris.

"Did the guys say when they'd be back?"

"Probably not for a while. They filled a wheelbarrow before they headed off into the words."

A day to relax and do nothing. Like almost every day since they arrived at the cabin.

Alissa scooped some of the eggs into her mouth. She would make breakfast last a while.

NATHAN UNWRAPPED THE coil of barbed wire around the tree trunk, circling it once, then continued to the next tree in line, keeping the strand four feet above the ground. Chris followed behind him, hammering two nails into the tree above and below the loop at an angle to anchor the strand in place. Kiera brought up the rear of the production line. Nathan had already stripped the labels off the old food cans they had used and punched a hole in each can an inch from the top rim. She tied two cans to the strand stretching between each tree and then covered the bottom of the can with pebbles and small rocks. Shithead took on the self-appointed role as protector of the realm, chasing every squirrel that threatened the safety of the group.

"Let's take a break," suggested Nathan.

The three of them sat down on an old tree that had fallen over and drank from their canteens. Shithead continued waging his one-dog war.

"Tell me again. What are we doing?" asked Chris.

"We're setting up an early warning system around the cabin."

"How do you figure that?"

Nathan gestured for Kiera to pass him one of the cans. When she did, he scooped up a handful of stones and tossed them inside. "If something gets caught in the barbed wire, it'll shake the cans." He jiggled it from side to side, allowing the stones to bang against the metal. "We know there are deaders approaching."

"Won't animals set it off?"

"Keeping the height at four feet will allow almost everything to pass underneath without disturbing the wire, except for deer and bears. Even then, once they tap the wire, they'll avoid it. Only deaders will be dumb enough to keep pushing against it, which will create a lot of noise."

"I guess." Chris did not sound convinced.

"Trust me, it'll work."

"Won't you have to be outside to hear it?" asked Kiera in all seriousness.

For a moment, Nathan had no answer. Chris made no attempt to hide his grin. He pointed to Kiera and then tapped his brow repeatedly. Kiera didn't see the gesture, her attention on Nathan waiting for an answer.

"Well... we'll be able to hear it from inside the cabin."

"The walls are insulated. And with all the noise inside we can't hear a thing outside."

"Yeah," teased Chris. "What about all the noise inside?"

Nathan scratched the bridge of his nose with his middle finger. "We really only need it at night so nothing can sneak up on us. I'll sleep with my window open."

Kiera's eyebrows crinkled. "Will you hear it over your snoring?"

Chris burst out laughing.

Kiera switched her gaze between Chris and Nathan. "Did I say something funny?"

"You're fine," answered Nathan. "Don't worry about it."

A few minutes of silence passed.

Kiera spoke first. "Uncle Nate, can I ask you a question?"

"Sure." He took another sip from his canteen.

"Why haven't you asked Alissa out?"

Chris snorted. Nathan choked on his water, which made Chris laugh out loud again.

It took a few seconds for Nathan to catch his breath. "Why do you ask?"

"It's obvious the two of you like each other."

"Well... yeah... we're friends."

"Please." Kiera dragged out the word in a dramatic expression of frustration. "I've seen the way the two of you look at each other. You know she'll say yes. All you have to do is ask."

"Yeah." Chris enjoyed Nathan's discomfort way too much. "All you have to do is ask."

"That's enough out of you." Nathan flashed his friend the evil eye.

"And if you're not interested in dating Alissa, then you should allow Uncle Chris to ask her out."

The grin drained from Chris' face. "What?"

Kiera turned to him. "I know you like her. Why else do you come over every night for dinner?"

Nathan grinned like the Cheshire Cat. "Why do you come over every night for dinner?"

"Because your mother is a good cook." Chris stood up. "And if we want to be back in time for dinner, we should get back to work."

"Nice save," Nathan whispered as Chris walked.

Not surprisingly, no one spoke for the remainder of the day.

Chapter Five

DICKSON DROVE EAST along Route 112 and kept to the speed limit to preserve fuel. The Hummer and Silverado made great vehicles for cutting cross country and pushing through hordes of deaders, but at the expense of being gas guzzlers. Several times they had come precariously close to running out, pulling into a gas station with the fuel gauge hovering below E. One time both the Hummer and the pick-up ran dry, forcing them to syphon gas from the other vehicles. They barely made it to the next service station. Ever since that day, Dickson didn't push as hard and, so far, they had no problems. It also helped that the convoy kept to the back roads, avoiding most of the deaders and providing greater opportunity to find fuel and supplies. Unfortunately, the last five stations they had come across, as well as the few vehicles they had encountered, were empty. The Hummer's gauge hovered above the E line.

Since entering eastern Vermont, and continuing into western New Hampshire, the number of deaders they had encountered dropped dramatically, except for when they crossed Interstate 89 that morning. The back road they traveled led them through an underpass beneath the highway, which avoided the bulk of the deaders. A few that had stumbled down the embankment attacked the convoy but were either avoided or quickly dispatched. Most of the living dead on the interstate weren't even aware they had passed. Dickson hoped their luck would hold until they reached Maine, though he doubted it.

"*Hey, boss.*" Carter's voice came over the radio. "*You there?*"

Dickson keyed the microphone. "What's up?"

"*I need to find a gas station soon, or we need to pull over and trade out, cuz my gas gauge has been below E for ten minutes.*"

"It would have been nice to know that ten minutes ago."

Joel leaned forward from the back seat. "There's the New Hampton Fire Department."

"What the fuck good does that do? We're not going to find gas there."

"No." Joel sounded much more contrite. "But it probably means we're entering a populated area, so we might find a gas station."

Dickson keyed the microphone. "The newbie says there should be a gas station up ahead."

"*What do you know? He's good for something after all.*"

"We'll see," answered Dickson. "If he's right, we'll stop in a minute. If not, the newbie can suck the gas from one tank to the other."

Carter laughed. "*He'll probably like it.*"

Dickson placed the radio back on the dashboard and glanced at Nora. "Where are we?"

"How do I know?"

"Read the fucking map, bitch."

Nora pulled it from the central console and opened it, searching for their location.

"Well?" barked Dickson.

"I... I haven't been keeping track of where we are."

"Fuck me."

Rebecca reached between the seats, yanked the map from Nora, and brought it in back with her.

"Hey," Nora protested.

"Shut up." Rebecca unfolded the map on her knees.

Nora turned to Dickson. "Are you going to let her—?"

"Fuck off. Let her do your job."

Rebecca scanned the map until she found New Hampton.

"We're approaching 93," whispered Joel.

"I know that."

Joel placed his hand on hers. She jerked her arm away. "Leave me alone."

The overpass for Route 93 came into view. Hundreds of deaders stumbled along the highway, and scores more staggered along the on/off ramps and the lanes of the road they were on. As they drove by, they turned toward the convoy and shambled toward it.

Dickson leaned back. "I need info."

"One second." Rebecca found the location and tapped her finger on the map. "According to this, there are several gas stations and places to eat on the other side of the interstate."

"Good."

Rebecca shook her head. "Not really. If there are this many deaders here, the rest areas are probably swarming with them."

As if on cue, Dickson slammed the brakes on the Hummer. Nora nearly hit the windshield, grabbing the dashboard at the last moment. Joel and Rebecca, not wearing their belts, slammed into the back seats. Behind him, Carter applied his brakes. The Silverado slid along the asphalt, coming to a stop three inches from the Hummer. Dickson didn't notice any of this, his attention drawn to what lay ahead of him.

A few hundred feet in front of them stood an Irving Oil and a Mobile gas station, a liquor store, and a Dunkin Donuts and other fast food restaurants. This place had been a rest stop for drivers and truckers. During the first few days of the outbreak, it had served as a safe haven for those stranded or seeking a break from the gridlock that paralyzed I-93. The spread of the outbreak this far north transformed the area into a hotbed of deader activity. Close to a thousand of them roamed the streets and parking lots, milled around the pumping stations, and wandered through the surrounding woods. When they heard the squeal of brakes, all milky white eyes focused on the vehicles, recognizing them as food.

The horde lumbered toward the convoy.

"Shit!"

Elaine, from the cargo van at the rear of the convoy, yelled over the radio. *"What's going on? Why have we stopped?"*

"Deaders," answered Carter. *"Hundreds of them blocking our path."*

"Do something."

Dickson grabbed the microphone. "Shut the fuck up. Let me think."

Rebecca's eyes connected with Joel and she mouthed, "We're all going to die."

ELAINE CHECKED HER sides mirrors. The deaders from the I-93 interchange had reached them and flowed around either side of the cargo van. A few dozen stopped at the side windows, scratching and biting at the glass to get to her. The rest passed by, focused on the real prize—Diana and her two children trapped in bed of the Chevy pick-up.

DIANA WATCHED THE deaders lumber toward them. She felt a stream of warm urine flow down her leg and fought back the urge to shit herself. Connie cried, even more terrified than her mother at the sight of the living dead. Brian threw his sister down onto the bed and covered her with his body.

"Mom, we have to get out here."

Crawling to the rear windows of the cab, Diana banged on the glass until Stratman slid open the window.

"What?"

"You have to get us out of here."

"No shit, bitch. I'm waiting for the boss."

"If you wait for him, we're all going to die."

Stratman slammed shut the window. Diana went to bang

on it again when a hand clutched her dress and pulled. She broke free and fell against the rear of the cab. Deaders swarmed around the pick-up bed, seven or eight deep. Scores of rotted hands reached through the open windows in the cap and clutched at her and Brian. A swarm of flies and hornets hovered around Diana and her children, with even more still feasting off the living dead. The hideous sight of ravaged and rotting faces mixed with the overpowering stench of decay made her retch. Connie screamed at the top of her lungs beneath her brother, her fear having switched to pure terror. Some of the tattered hands reaching for Brian clasped on his arms and yanked, threatening to pull him off his sister.

"Mom, I need help."

Diana crawled over to assist her son. A hand entwined itself in her long hair and tugged, knocking Diana onto her back, then pulled her across the bed. She raised her eyes and saw the gaping mouth of a deader through the window only inches away.

Watching what went on from his rearview mirror, Stratman keyed the radio. "We gotta get out of here now!"

"*WE GOTTA GET out of here now!*"

Dickson didn't bother responding. His mind had gone blank under pressure.

"Go through them," ordered Nora.

"There are too many. They'll box us in and then we're fucked."

"What about back tracking?" suggested Joel.

"Too many behind us."

"You're all assholes." Rebecca leaned forward and pointed to the left where a park-and-ride lot stood. "Go that way."

"It's fucking parking lot."

"There's a road running behind it. With luck it'll take us around all this."

Dickson spun around to face her. "What if it's a dead end?"

"It's better than staying here and being eaten alive," she snapped.

Being yelled at snapped Dickson back to reality. He picked up the radio and keyed the microphone. "There's a road to our left. Follow me."

Spinning the steering wheel hard to the left, Dickson made a U-turn, bounced over the curb, and veered past the park-and-ride onto the road leading to the Department of Transportation compound.

CARTER STARTED TO follow Dickson until the latter circled back and headed down the side road. He then got his first full view of what lie ahead of them. Deaders flowed out of every parking lot along the road, converging on them, hundreds of them stretching across the width of the road and packed several layers deep.

Gunning the Silverado, Carter fell in behind Dickson.

DIANA REACHED OUT with her right hand and jammed it against the bed of the pick-up, preventing herself from being dragged to the deader's mouth. She spun around, placed her knees against the interior wall, and kicked. A sharp pain shot through her head as she pushed herself away from the deader, which still clutched a fistful of her hair in its hand. No sooner had she broke free when the living dead on the other side clutched at her through the windows. Diana scrambled back to the center of the bed, slapping away the outstretched hands.

At that moment, the pick-up lurched forward. Most of the hands disappeared as the pick-up drove away. A few grabbed for the canopy, hanging on desperately for a few seconds before their grips loosened and they dropped off. All except one deader, a large man in a road construction uniform, that had a firm grip on Brian's right arm. When the truck accelerated, the road crew deader fell to the side, dragging Brian across the bed until he crashed into the canopy. A loud snap accompanied Brian's scream of pain as the bone shattered and punched through the skin. As the pick-up distanced itself from the horde, he rolled around, howling in agony.

"About fucking time," Elaine mumbled as she pushed her way through the horde and turned left at the park-and-ride.

The convoy reached the end of the lot and entered the DOT compound, passing by the garage. Five orange-colored dump trucks sat parked off to the left.

Dickson punched the steering wheel. "It's a fucking dead end."

"No, it's not." Rebecca leaned forward and pointed directly ahead of them. "That road should take us out of here."

"You better be right or I'm feeding you to those things."

Dickson accelerated and headed for the opposite end of the compound. Sure enough, the road extended into the woods beyond before turning back toward the main road. They might make it yet.

The Silverado bucked. The engine stuttered and the engine bucked again.

Carter stared at the dashboard. "No. No. No. No."

The Silverado bucked a final time and stalled.

"What's going on?" asked Williamson.

Carter grabbed the radio and jumped out of the cab, leaving the door open behind him. "I ran out of gas. Elaine, pull up beside me so we can unload into your van."

"We don't have enough time," she replied.

"We do if you haul ass." Carter popped open the lid to the bed and banged on the side of the Silverado, motioning for Williamson to join him.

Stratman parked the Chevy on their left, jumped out, and raced around to the passenger door. Opening it, he began to load as many supplies as possible into the front seat. Elaine pulled up along the right, stopping so the rear doors were in front of the pick-up's bed. Carter whipped them open and began transferring the Silverado's load into the van.

"Brian needs help," pleaded Diana.

"We're a little busy."

"His arm is broken."

"Bitch, if you don't shut up, I'll break his other one. Let me know when those things get close or I'll leave the three of you here."

"STOP THE CAR." Rebecca stared out the rear window. "The pick-up stalled."

"Damn it." Dickson slowed and checked his side mirror, watching as Carter and Stratman unloaded the Silverado and packed the supplies in the other vehicles.

"Should we help them?" asked Nora.

"Not enough time," he lied, not wanting to get that close to the horde. "They'll be fine."

THE THREE MEN continued unloading as much as they could from the back of the Silverado.

"How close?" Carter yelled out.

Diana glanced up from tending to Brian's arm. "About a hundred and fifty feet."

"I'm full." Stratman slammed the passenger door. "Do you guys need help?"

"No time. Get ready to haul ass out of here."

Stratman climbed back into his pick-up, standing on the running board.

Carter gave the back of the van a quick scan. He had forgotten some of the ammo. He rushed back to the Silverado and rummaged through the remaining supplies for the boxes.

"Seventy-five feet," called out Diana.

Stratman blared the horn, attracting the attention of some of the deaders, but not enough. Half still closed in on Carter.

He found the boxes of ammunition and waved for Williamson. When Williamson approached, he loaded into his arms as many boxes as the kid could carry and then pushed him toward the van.

"Get in back and close it up. Tell Elaine to be ready to move."

"Less than ten yards." Diana banged the cap to get Carter's attention. "Hurry."

Carter picked up a box of ammo in each hand and started for the van when a deader in a waitress uniform snarled and grabbed his left shoulder. He jumped to the right, breaking its grip, knocking the deader off balance. Carter moved around it when another deader, naked and with its abdomen torn open, surged forward. It tackled Carter. Both fell backwards into the van's bay. Carter dropped the boxes of ammo and wrapped his hands around the deader's throat, preventing it from getting too close. A dozen more deaders closed in on the van.

Williamson unholstered the Beretta he had taken from Rebecca, aimed at the deader's head, and fired. The bullet missed, punching into the forehead of the deader behind it.

"Try hitting it next time," said Carter.

Williamson moved closer and pumped two rounds into the naked deader's head, blasting away everything above the neck. Carter pushed the carcass off him and rolled into the back of the van. Three more deaders tried to crawl in after him. Carter rushed forward, pushing Williamson along with him. He tapped the back of Elaine's seat.

"Go."

Elaine slammed her foot on the gas pedal and the van lurched forward, spilling the three deaders and several boxes of supplies out the back. Once he got his footing, Carter made his way to the rear and closed the double doors.

Deaders surged around the Chevy, reaching through the open windows at Diana and her children, driven to a frenzy by the smell of blood from Brian's compound fracture. She covered her son with her own body and kicked the cab. "Let's get out of here."

"Not until I'm sure Carter's safe."

When the cargo van pulled away with everyone safely on board, Diana yelled, "He's okay. Now can we go?"

"All right. All right."

Stratman pulled away, leaving the rest of the deaders stumbling after the convoy.

"HERE THEY COME," warned Rebecca.

"I see them." Dickson waited until the others got close before driving.

The road turned right and soon came back out onto the main road on the other side of the gas stations. Most of the deaders staggered off to their right, following the horde into the DOT compound, leaving the left clear except for a handful of living dead. Dickson veered to the left and headed east along the main road, getting out of the area as fast as possible.

Chapter Six

CHRIS STAYED FOR dinner. Because he, Nathan, and Kiera had worked hard all day, Miriam defrosted and cooked some of the steaks Paul had stored in the freezer as well as two hamburger patties, one for Little Stevie and the other for Shithead. After everything had been cleaned, they all sat around the living room chatting and drinking coffee while Little Stevie played Nintendo Switch.

Alissa blew on her coffee to cool it off a bit. "Kiera told me about this afternoon."

Nathan and Chris stared at each nervously and turned their gaze onto Kiera. Chris asked, "What did she tell you?"

"That you spent all day working on a perimeter fence."

Nathan almost sighed with relief. "We did. We set it up around the entire cabin."

"Isn't it a single strand of barbed wire with cans filled with rocks attached?" asked Steve.

"Yeah."

"How will that stop the deaders?"

"It's not supposed to stop them. If they get caught in the barbed wire, they'll shake the cans and warn us deaders are in the area."

Steve thought about it for a moment. "Wouldn't somebody have to be outside to hear it?"

Chris snorted. Kiera giggled. Nathan's face became stern.

Steve seemed confused. "Did I say something wrong?"

"No," answered Nathan.

"It's been pointed out to him already." Kiera had a shit-eaten smirk on her face.

Steve opted to ignore the little secret between the three of them. "I'm more worried about the driveway leading up here."

"Why?" Alissa had not even thought about that before now.

"The road is wide open." Steve drank some coffee. "Anyone can come right up it."

"Why can't we string some barbed wire across it like in the woods?" Miriam asked.

Steve placed the cup down on the coaster. "I'm not worried about deaders so much as the living."

"We haven't seen any living since we got here." Nathan sounded dismissive.

"Yet." No one responded, letting Steve's response set in, so he continued. "Anybody could come up that driveway and be sitting out in front of the cabin before we realized it. If it's a car with one or two people in it, we're safe. But if it's a biker gang, we may not be so lucky."

Nathan shook his head. "I don't think a biker gang—"

"He's right," interrupted Chris. "It's our weakest point. If a pack of deaders follow a deer up here we're screwed."

"How likely is that?" Alissa asked.

Chris shrugged.

"She does bring up a point," said Steve. "No one has been out there for weeks since you went to get the medical supplies for my leg."

"That was fun," Kiera cut in.

Miriam rolled her eyes. "Oh, dear God."

"As far as we know," continued Steve, "every deader in New England could be milling around North Conway. Or they all wandered off, leaving the city as empty as an early Sunday morning."

Nathan agreed. "We should do a recon of the surrounding area tomorrow so we know what's out there."

Kiera straightened in her chair and her eyes opened wide. "Can I go?"

"Sure," said Chris.

"No!" added Miriam.

"Come on," Kiera pleaded. "Why not?"

"Because last time you almost got yourself killed."

"I saved everyone."

"I said no, young lady."

Kiera made a frumpy face and crossed her arms across her chest.

"She was a big help last time." Nathan gently prodded Miriam. "The experience does her good. Besides, we're not getting out or going into any stores. We'll be driving around getting a feel for the area."

Miriam hesitated. "Are you sure she'll be safe?"

"I will be." Kiera almost shouted the words.

Alissa tapped Kiera's arm to warn her to be quiet. "Don't worry. I'm going along so I can guarantee she'll be fine."

Kiera stared at her mother with large saucer-plate eyes. It reminded Alissa of the way Archer stared at her when he begged for treats.

Miriam said nothing, internally struggling with her decision. "Steve, what do you think?"

"As long as she's with the three of them she'll be fine."

"Okay," Miriam sighed. "You can go."

"Yes!" Kiera jumped out of her seat, ran around the table, and hugged her mother. "I promise, you won't regret this."

"I do already."

"Do you want me to go with you?" Steve asked.

"We're fine," Nathan responded.

"Thanks," added Chris.

"I feel useless sitting around her all day doing nothing. I want to pitch in."

"When you're back on your feet you can." Alissa's voice had that reassuring tone she had practiced so often while being a nurse.

"Do you need me to go with you?" Miriam asked.

"No!" Kiera spoke too quickly and received another tap on the arm from Alissa.

"We're fine," she said. "Thanks for the offer."

Miriam nodded. "I'll stay here with Steve and keep an eye on Little Stevie."

"Great." Little Stevie stayed focused on his game. "You two will be upstairs all day and leave me alone again."

Kiera placed her hands over her ears. "TMI. TMI."

Alissa stifled a laugh.

Nathan and Chris stared at each other, finally realizing what Little Stevie meant when they noticed Miriam turning fifty shades of red. Steve did not help matters any by giving the two men a thumbs up.

Miriam pushed her seat back and headed for the kitchen. "I'm going to do the dishes."

Steve chuckled. "You did them already."

She stopped at the door and glared at her husband, though she smiled flirtatiously. "One more word out of you and I'll go with them tomorrow."

Steve pretended to close a zipper across his lips and saluted his wife. Everyone laughed except Little Stevie, whose interest had returned to his video game, and Kiera who no longer wanted to be a part of this conversation.

Chapter Seven

DICKSON STOPPED FOR the night at a junkyard fifteen miles from New Hampton. It offered the perfect place to lay low—off the main road so passing deaders wouldn't notice them, a gated compound, and scores of wrecked cars so their own vehicles blended in. As a plus, the only deader inside happened to be the owner, which they took down silently and quickly. As Carter built a campfire in the center of the yard where it could not be seen, and Elaine and Nora along with Williamson inventoried what supplies were saved from the Silverado, Dickson went to check on the Taylor kid.

He found the family gathered around the bed of the Chevy, with mom and son sitting on the tailgate. The deaders had fucked up his arm bad, with three inches of the fractured humerus poking through the skin. Dickson remembered breaking his arm as a boy. It had been the worst pain he had ever experienced. This must hurt like a son of a bitch. The kid panted heavily and groaned every time anyone touched his arm. At least he didn't cry like some sissy. His mother sat behind him, cradling him and telling him everything would be all right. Stratman hovered nearby, watching nervously as Rebecca examined the wound. Joel and Connie stood back and watched.

"Can you fix it?" Diana asked through her tears.

"I'm checking," Rebecca answered.

Dickson strolled up and peered over Rebecca's shoulder. "I didn't know you were a nurse."

"I'm not. After college I spent a few years as a flight attendant and they trained us in first aid. I've set broken bones before but nothing this severe."

"What does he need?"

"He needs to get to a hospital."

"Good luck with that." Dickson ignored her angry glare. "What do you need to fix him up?"

"I'm going to need three pieces of wood or metal to hold the bone in place, preferably no longer than his upper arm. I'll also need bandages for the wound and enough gauze to cover it. Something to stitch up the wound if you have it. And the strongest pain meds you have."

Dickson snapped his fingers, catching Stratman's attention. "You heard her. See if we have any of those supplies."

As Stratman headed for the other vehicles, Dickson turned to Joel. "Take the girl and find some splints for his arm."

"What should I be looking for?"

"Something to make a splint out of, asshole. You're supposedly smart. You'll figure it out."

Joel's expression faltered. For a second, Dickson thought he might cry. Taking Connie by the hand, Joel led her into the junkyard.

Meanwhile, Rebecca tended to Brian. She patted him on the leg. "You're lucky in one respect."

"How?" asked Brian.

"If the bone had punctured the artery, you'd have been dead an hour ago."

"Lucky me," Brian grunted through clenched teeth.

"I'm going to set the bone."

"Will it hurt?" he asked.

"Even more than when you broke it."

"Fuck."

"Brian." Diana chastised him from force of habit.

"Sorry."

Rebecca caught Diana's attention. "I'm going to need you

to hold your son tight."

Diana nodded.

She glanced up at Dickson. "I need your help as well."

"Sure." He moved closer.

"When I tell you to, pull on Brian's arm. Not too hard, though. I need an inch or two at most so I can push the bones back together."

"Gotcha."

Rebecca tapped Brian's ankle. "Are you ready?"

"No." His attempt at a laugh ended with him wincing.

"On the count of three. One. Two. Three."

Dickson pulled on Brian's arm as Rebecca pushed the extruded portion of the humerus back into place. The teenager screamed at the top of his lungs. His body convulsed for a moment and went limp.

"Is he...?" Diana couldn't finish her question.

"No," Rebecca responded. She reached out and rubbed Diana's shoulder. "He passed out from shock. It's better for him. He'll sleep through it."

"How's the bone going to heal?" she asked.

"Poorly. If he were in a hospital, they'd probably screw the bones together so they could heal properly. I don't have that capability. Sorry."

"What does that mean?"

"It means his right arm will probably be crippled for life, or until we can find a doctor who can fix it."

Diana cried again and hugged Brian. He groaned even while unconscious.

Stratman arrived a minute later with an armful of medical supplies that he placed on the tailgate. "Here you go."

Rebecca thumbed through them. A bottle of rubbing alcohol. A bottle of Advil. "Do you have any needles and thread?"

"We couldn't find any."

"Shit." Rebecca thought for a second. "What about Crazy Glue?"

"No."

She thumbed through the supplies. They had only one roll of tape and gauze. "Is this all?"

"For the tape, yes. There's more gauze."

"We'll need it. Do you have any duct tape?"

"I might have some in the Chevy."

"Could you get it for me?"

Stratman nodded. "Sure thing."

Rebecca opened the rubbing alcohol and held the bottle over the wound. "Hold him down."

Diana pinned Brian's shoulders against her chest. Rebecca poured a third of the alcohol along the wound. The teenager grimaced and moaned. When finished, she patted down the area around the wound with a sterile pad and, when dried, sealed the wound shut with strips of surgical tape.

Dickson observed the process until Carter and Williamson came up to him. He ushered them away so Rebecca could work.

"What were you able to salvage from the Silverado?"

"Not much, unfortunately." Carter hesitated. "Five packs of bottled water and seven crates of canned food. Twenty rolls of toilet paper…."

"Who the fuck needs that much toilet paper during an apocalypse?" snapped Dickson.

"…only one box of medical supplies, most of it gauze. We lost the box filled with prescription meds."

"What about ammo?"

Carter and Williamson avoided Dickson's gaze. "We left most of it behind."

"Fuck!" Dickson walked away and turned his back on them. Now they would have to restock everything they had spent the last two months gathering. The shitty part was they would have to accomplish this with only limited ammunition. He spun around to face his men.

"Why didn't you save the important stuff like ammunition?

That's what we needed."

"Boss, come on." Carter at least had the balls to stand up for himself. "We did the best we could. Considering the horde of deaders coming after us, we're lucky we saved anything."

Dickson glared at Williamson. "What about you?"

Williamson's gaze switched between the two men before he finally lowered his eyes and pointed at Carter. "What he said."

Dickson wanted to kick their asses but decided against it. They might be assholes, but he needed them. "Grab some of the food and see if the girls have the fire ready. Help them with the cooking."

"Sure thing, boss." Carter slapped Williamson on the arm and the two ran off, glad they would receive no ass kicking.

Dickson went back to the Chevy. Rebecca finished up with Brian's broken arm. She had wrapped gauze tightly around it and held it in place with a strip of duct tape Stratman had brought her. Joel and Connie had found three pieces of metal that Rebecca used as splints, securing them in place with more duct tape. When she finished, she stood and moved beside Diana.

"He'll be fine."

"Are you sure?"

Rebecca nodded. "He'll be in a lot of pain for a while, but that can't be helped. I'll change the dressing every day to make sure it doesn't get infected."

Diana forced a smile. She clutched Rebecca's hand and squeezed tight. "I don't know how to thank you."

"No need to. We help each other out."

Dickson motioned for Rebecca to follow and led her far enough from the Chevy so the others could not be heard.

"Is the kid really going to be okay?"

"His arm won't heal properly under these circumstances and he's going to be in a lot of pain for weeks, but as long as he doesn't develop an infection he'll live."

"That's good."

"Do you really care?"

Dickson ignored the insult. "What do you need to help him recover?"

"Painkillers and anti-biotics."

"We'll have to do another supply run soon since we lost most of our stash today. We'll get the meds you need when we do."

"Thank you."

"You did good today." He meant the compliment with sincerity.

"I did?"

Dickson nodded. "You got us out of that jam at the interstate and you fixed up the kid. I appreciate it."

The compliment took Rebecca aback. "Thanks."

Dickson moved in close so he could speak quietly into her ear. "But if you keep mouthing off to me, I'm going to bitch slap you so hard you'll be the one needing medical care. Understood?"

Rebecca gulped and nodded.

Dickson gently patted her on the cheek. "Good girl."

He strolled off and let Rebecca tend to the kid. Right now, he needed something to eat and to plan out how they were going to resupply.

Chapter Eight

Alissa, Nathan, and Kiera stood at the dining room table making sure they had everything they needed for the recon. Chris had brought Shithead with him to go along for the ride. The dog lay curled up on the sofa until Archer came along. The cat meowed once. Shithead jumped off, avoiding contact with the small but mean creature, and moved over near the humans as the Archer took his rightful place on the couch.

Alissa and Nathan each had a main weapon, a back-up sidearm, and a melee weapon. Chris had his own and had already placed them in one of the cars. Each of them, including Kiera, had a backpack with extra ammo, three plastic bottles of water, three protein bars, and a small medical kit.

"Don't I get a weapon?" Kiera asked.

"I put a knife in your bag," Nathan answered.

"Do you think that's safe?" Miriam seemed concerned.

"Would you rather have her out there unarmed?"

"I'd rather not have her out there at all."

"Mom." Kiera whined the word and turned to Alissa for support.

"I understand how you feel, but she needs to learn how to defend herself for the future."

"Besides," added Nathan. "We're only driving around to get an idea of the number of deaders in the area. If we find any, we're going to avoid them."

"I know. I'm being a mother."

"A good mother," added Alissa.

"I can go?" Kiera's voice rose an octave in anticipation.

"Yes."

"You're the best." Kiera hugged her mother then stepped over to Alissa. "Can I get a gun?"

"No." Alissa and Miriam answered simultaneously.

"Are we ready?" asked Nathan.

"All we need is Chris," Alissa scanned the living room. "Where is he?"

Miriam pointed to the deck. "He stepped outside after he got here."

Alissa crossed the room and slid open the door to the deck. Chris stood at the railing, studying the eastern horizon with a pair of binoculars.

"Did you suddenly decide to take up bird watching?"

"I wish." Chris lowered the binoculars and pointed in the direction he had been studying. "I noticed that on the way over and wanted to check it out."

Alissa saw black smoke rising on the other side of the hills. She recognized the color and density as belonging to a multi-alarm fire. Only this smoke stretched for miles, blanketing the horizon.

"Oh my God."

"That's what I thought when I noticed it this morning." Chris handed her the binoculars. "You can't see much other than smoke."

Alissa examined the ridge. The flames came from the valley on the opposite side. Occasionally, a finger of fire would shoot up over the crest, staying in view for a few seconds before settling down.

"Which direction is it heading?" Alissa asked.

"I can't tell. What's on the other side?"

"Not much." Alissa handed back the binoculars. "Mostly a state forest that runs into Maine."

"Shit!"

"What's wrong?"

"We haven't had any rain since we got here two months ago. There's no moisture in the ground. If that fire is in the forest, there'll be no stopping it."

"Should we be preparing to bug out?"

Chris shook his head. "Not yet. It could be moving in the other direction. We should be okay as long as it doesn't crest the ridge or follow the road around to where we are."

"Should we tell the others?"

"Not yet. Let's check it out first." Chris ushered Alissa inside the cabin where the others waited.

"What took you so long?" Nathan asked, a slight tinge of jealousy in his voice.

"We were talking." Alissa removed her weapons from the table, attaching the holster and knife belt around her waist. She then slung the backpack over one shoulder and her Mossberg shotgun over the other. "Are we ready?"

The others responded in the affirmative.

"Let's go."

They followed her out, Shithead especially happy to be anywhere the cat was not. Miriam stopped Kiera long enough to give her a hug. Once outside, Chris and Alissa picked the Ram and Nathan and Kiera chose the Land Rover, loading their gear inside.

Five minutes later, the two vehicles drove off the mountain road, turned right onto Route 302, and headed toward North Conway.

Chapter Nine

D ICKSON'S PEOPLE HIT the road an hour and a half after sunrise. Williamson rode with Stratman and Carter with Elaine. Before leaving, Dickson noted the junk yard's location on the map and had Carter secure the front gate with a chain and lock. He wanted to keep this place for himself in case they needed it as a hiding place or to scavenge for spare parts. Dickson led the convoy northeast along Route 113.

This time Rebecca held the map and navigated from the back seat because he needed someone with a good head on their shoulders who didn't fold under pressure. She would warn him before the convoy reached populated areas or locales that could be possible hot spots so they didn't have any unexpected and almost fatal incidents, like in New Hampton yesterday, and to be on the lookout for places where they could attempt to resupply.

After an hour on the road, Rebecca leaned forward, still clutching the map in her hand. "Be careful. We'll be entering Conway in a few minutes. Beyond that is North Conway, the largest city in the area."

"Thanks." Picking up the radio, Dickson relayed the information to the others.

"How far are we from Maine?"

"It's a few miles from here if you stay on this road," Rebecca responded.

"Isn't that where we want to go?" asked Nora.

"It is." Dickson thought for a moment. "Let's check out this area first. We might be able to replenish what we lost."

CHRIS HEADED ALONG Route 302 East toward the northern approaches to North Conway, every once in awhile glancing over to the curtain of smoke rising from the other side of the ridge.

"I'd pay more attention to the road," warned Alissa.

"There's nobody out here."

"No, but there is wildlife. If you wind up hitting a moose, the kids are never going to let you live it down."

"You're right." Chris focused on the road. He hated the silence, especially because of that one issue that hung over their heads. Chris had been attracted to Alissa since he first met her and, if he picked up her vibes correctly, she liked him in return. He had ignored them these past few weeks. That wasn't true. He had thought a lot about the two of them becoming involved but always avoided bringing it up, not wanting to stir the pot with Nathan, and not wanting to deal with the rejection, and embarrassment, if she said no. Playing out the scenario in his mind was more fulfilling than bringing it out into the open. That luxury ended yesterday when Kiera raised the subject.

"So," Chris began hesitantly. "Are you and Nathan... a thing?"

Alissa stared at him like he had farted in church during a moment of silence. Chris instantly regretted opening his mouth.

"A thing?"

"Well... I meant—"

"A thing? Are we sixteen?"

"Sorry." Chris wished they would run into a pack of deaders. "I was trying to make conversation."

"It sounds like you're trying to ask me out."

Chris glanced over and fixed on her eyes, hoping to see

some interest or humor in them. They displayed no emotion, except maybe frustration. Oh God, please let a moose be around the next corner.

"I can't believe you're asking me out."

"I'm not asking you out," he protested too quickly and forcefully.

"Then why did you ask if Nathan and I were a *thing*?" The way Alissa emphasized the last two words made him want to shrink into the seat.

"Let's drop the subject."

"You brought it up."

"Please?"

"No." Alissa remained adamant.

Luck favored Chris. As they approached North Conway, a road branched off to the north and into the valley where the fire raged. He stopped.

"Where does that go?"

"Route 16? It'll take you to Berlin. Why?"

"I think that's the road the fire's on. We should check that out while we're here."

"Okay," agreed Alissa. "But this is not—"

Chris turned the vehicle north as he handed her the radio. "Let Nathan know what we're up to."

Chris almost sighed with relief when Alissa dropped the conversation and called Nathan. He continued along Route 16, rolling down the driver's window. The smell of burning wood grew overpowering with each mile they drove. Every few minutes, the tip of flames could be seen behind the tree line, illuminating the heavy black smoke that blocked out the sky above them. He heard the roar of the fire even at this distance, sounding like a nightmarish furnace.

"We should turn around," suggested Alissa. "I don't like this."

"Neither do I, but we need to know what we're... Jesus fucking Christ."

As they turned the bend near Wildcat Mountain the con-flagration came into view less than a mile away. The forest on both sides of the road burned furiously, from the shoulder all the way up to the tops of the ridges. A wall of orange-yellow fire blocked the valley, flickering over a hundred feet in height. The local wildlife scurried to escape certain death. A black bear with its three cubs ran past the vehicle, ignoring the humans, concerned only with saving its young.

The swarm of deaders made the scene even more surreal. Attracted by the noise and motion, nearly twenty of the living dead stumbled toward the inferno, oblivious to the fate that awaited them. Chris opened the door, stepped out, and raised the binoculars. The deader closest to the fire, a female State trooper with long hair down its back, staggered toward the flames. Swirls of white smoke from the intense heat formed on its hair and clothes. The deader pressed ahead. It ignited as it crossed the fire line yet refused to turn around, its primordial brain convinced the roar of the conflagration meant food. Chris wondered if it was aware of the agony its body endured, the burning of flesh, the frying of organs, the searing away of muscles. The Trooper deader slowed and swayed, finally collapsing face first onto the softened pavement, and yet it still flayed its limbs, not yet completely charred. Despite witnessing the demise of one of their own, the others pushed ahead, one by one disappearing into the fire.

Nathan stepped up beside Chris as Kiera joined Alissa.

"Can I see?" he asked.

Chris handed over the binoculars so Nathan could watch the deaders perform their walk of death.

A large, smoking pine tree on the left side of the road sud-denly caught fire, becoming completely engulfed within seconds.

"Wait a minute," said Kiera. "If the wind is blowing from behind us, why is the fire moving in our direction?"

"That's not wind," answered Nathan, still watching the

deaders. "The fire is consuming so much oxygen it's sucking in the air around it."

"I don't like it here," said Alissa. "Let's go."

Chris held up a finger. "One minute."

Nathan lowered the binoculars. "I wonder how many deaders have been sucked into that thing?"

"Hopefully most of the deaders in North Conway have been drawn here, leaving the city open for us to scavenge."

"We should check it out."

Another pine tree smoked and ignited. Alissa banged the roof of the vehicle. "Can we go?"

Chris waved his hand dismissively, thankfully not seeing the glare from Alissa. "Since you're behind us, you lead and we'll follow."

"Sounds good." Nathan tapped the roof to get Kiera's attention. "Come on, kid. We're out of here."

"I'm not a kid," she protested as she headed back to the vehicle.

"Okay, young lady."

"You could call me by my name, you know."

Chris let the two of them banter and slid back into his vehicle. Alissa climbed in beside him.

"It's time we get out of here," he said.

Alissa leaned over and punched him in his upper right arm.

Chris rubbed the spot. "What was that for?"

Alissa said nothing and folded her arms across her chest.

Chapter Ten

As Dickson's convoy approached North Conway, he came to a stop. A few dozen deaders were visible on the main road, the side streets, and parking lots, yet not in enough proximity or numbers to pose an immediate threat.

"How big is this town?" he asked Rebecca.

"It's the largest in this part of the state. It's a major tourist destination."

"Nervous?" asked Nora.

"Cautious." The venom with which he spoke the word caused Nora to shrink away. "I don't want a repeat of yesterday's clusterfuck."

"There's a back road that parallels the main one. It's up ahead. That one's probably a safer bet than going straight through town. It also brings us close to the local hospital."

"You navigate."

Dickson drove on. A deader in military fatigues and with no lower jaw crossed the Hummer's path. Dickson accelerated, knocking it over. The others behind him swerved around the body.

Rebecca tapped the driver's seat. "There's the library. Turn left here."

Dickson veered the Hummer onto West Side Street. They followed that road until Rebecca told them to turn right on River Road. Half a mile later, Dickson pulled over to the shoulder.

"Is everything okay?" asked Nora.

"I don't know." Dickson pointed in front of them.

A small two-lane bridge spanned the Saco River. A flock of crows sat on the cement railing along the left side, diving down beneath the bridge and flying back to their perch with meat dangling from their beaks. Every time the crows dropped down, they disturbed a swarm of flies and wasps that flew above the expanse before settling down again.

"What the fuck is that?" asked Nora.

"Only one way to find out." Dickson picked up the radio. "Carter, grab your weapon and get up here. Everyone else, be ready to move in case we have to get out of here in a hurry."

Dickson climbed out of the Hummer and moved closer to the bridge, stopping fifty feet away. Carter joined him a few seconds later.

"What's up?"

Dickson motioned to the bridge. "Any idea what that is?"

"Not a fucking clue."

Raising their weapons, the two men closed in on the bridge, staying in the center of the road. Once on the span, they moved over to the railing. The crows flew off, squawking in protest. The two men leaned over the side.

Carter whistled between his teeth. "You've got to be fucking kidding."

They stared down at an ungodly dam. At least one hundred bodies stacked up around the pilings and stretched underneath the span, their limbs entwined, broken tree branches serving as makeshift rebar to hold the corpses together. That was not correct. The dam did not consist of just corpses but also the living dead, their bodies still moving, unable to break free. A mass of smaller branches and litter covered the outer bodies.

"What happened here?" asked Dickson.

"A mass of them must have wandered out onto the ice, probably chasing a deer, and broke through. For some reason they all clogged up here and melded together."

"They weren't chasing deer." Dickson pointed to one of the

motionless deaders resting on top of the heap. "That one has a bullet wound to the chest and half its head has been blown off. There's a lot more like that."

"You're saying someone else killed these things."

"More than likely several people. They may still be in the area, so let's be on our guard."

"I'll tell the others." Carter motioned over the side of the bridge. "What should we do about them?"

"Nothing. If they haven't freed themselves by now, I doubt they ever will." Dickson moved away from the guardrail. "Besides, this town is too big. I don't plan on staying around, only long enough to get a new ride and some supplies. Come on."

Once back in the Hummer, Dickson explained what had happened. When Carter got back into the Chevy, Dickson drove off, leading the convoy to the hospital.

ALISSA KEPT HER Mossberg between her legs, the barrel pointing at the floorboard, ready to be used at a moment's notice. Chris thought she seemed overly cautious, noting they would have enough time to get away or prepare to engage if they came across any deaders. Alissa didn't care. After what she had experienced at Mass General and on the streets of Boston, she could not take enough precautions to make her feel secure.

They entered Intervale, the town adjacent to North Conway, passing by the scenic vista and the Intervale Motel. A handful of deaders staggered north toward the conflagration, all of them crippled in one form or another, limping on bad legs or crawling along the pavement. One of the limpers had its abdomen ripped open, leaving a trail of congealed blood and gore that stretched for half a mile, and dragging its unraveled intestines behind it. The same situation greeted them as they entered North Conway. They drove for half a mile and spotted no more than twenty deaders.

Chris stopped on a section of road surrounded by four hotels and stepped out.

"What are you doing?" barked Alissa.

"I want to check something." Raising his weapon, he fired a three-round burst into the air.

Alissa leaned over and yelled out the driver's side. "Have you lost your mind?"

Chris ignored her and scanned the area. After a few seconds, he fired three more rounds. Nathan pulled up alongside him. Kiera rolled down the window.

"What are you doing?" asked Nathan.

"Experimenting. What do you see?"

At one time, the area had been a war zone. The hotels were peppered with bullet holes and smeared with dry blood. The parking lots in front of each building had been killing fields. Scores of vehicles, including police cars and National Guard ordinance, littered the lots, some still pristine and neatly parked, others abandoned with their doors open, the interiors covered with blood and rotting body parts. Hundreds of corpses lay scattered across the pavement, a few of them belonging to deaders taken down in combat. Most had been victims of the outbreak, people overrun by the horde and devoured to such an extent none of them reanimated. Their bodies showed months of decay. Even the birds and insects did not bother feeding off them. The destruction spilled out onto the street.

"It's carnage," said Alissa.

The bloated corpse of a woman sat along the curb farther down the road, its face having been stripped clean of flesh, its extended stomach pushing through the soiled bathrobe it wore. Chris fired a single round into its abdomen. The body popped like a balloon, spilling its liquified interior onto the street, which poured into the nearby storm drain.

Kiera leaned out the window and vomited.

"Cut it out." Nathan's voice seethed with anger.

The gunfire had attracted a score of deaders that stumbled toward them, hobbled like the others they had encountered. Others howled from inside closed rooms, scratching at the glass, having been trapped inside before turning.

"Are you trying to get us killed?" demanded Alissa.

"That's my point." Chris slung his weapon over his shoulder. "We should have a horde of them bearing down on us. We don't."

Kiera wiped her mouth. "So?"

"This place had been a major refugee point until the dead took over. Remember what happened a few weeks ago at the hospital? Rather than be swarmed by deaders, none are left. They all chased the forest fire."

How could Alissa forget. Her and Nathan had almost died there getting the supplies for Steve's surgery. She climbed out of the vehicle and studied the area.

"You're right, but you're still crazy."

"I won't argue that." Chris flashed Alissa a flirtatious smile that she ignored. "At least we know we're safe from being overrun by deaders for a while."

"What about those coming from nearby towns?" Nathan asked, his tone no longer aggressive.

"I hate to admit Chris is right," said Alissa. "The other towns nearby are small and were already evacuated on our way up here. I doubt we have anything to worry about."

"We should probably check out the rest of town to be sure." When no one responded, Chris added, "Agree?"

Alissa shrugged. "Yeah."

"Okay." Nathan thought a moment. "I'll take the lead."

Chris smiled. "Roger that."

As Chris and Alissa climbed back into their vehicle, Nathan pulled in front and headed deeper into North Conway.

Everyone averted their gaze as they passed Memorial Hospital, none of them wanting to remember the nightmare they had endured there.

The rest of the town seemed the same as the northern portion. Every place that had been used as a refugee camp showed evidence of a massacre. The only deaders still in the area were cripples crawling toward the fire. By the time they reached the southern outskirts and passed the mineral springs, the number of mobile deaders had increased, but not by much, seven or eight of them stumbling north. They approached the two vehicles. Nathan ran over the closest.

"You were right about the deaders coming in from other towns," Nathan's voice came over the radio. *"Should we turn back?"*

Alissa picked up the radio. "No need. The back road to the cabin is up ahead. Turn onto West Side Road."

Nathan turned when they came to the street and accelerated, with Chris keeping pace, heading back to the cabin, and leaving the deaders far behind.

THE MOMENT DICKSON pulled into the parking lot of Memorial Hospital it became obvious that someone else had been here before them and left one hell of a mess. Corpses lay scattered around the parking lot in front of the shattered main entrance. The building out front, the one designated as the Orthopedics Center, resembled a war zone. Scores of bodies of the living dead lined the front wall, some with crippling head wounds, others having been run over by a large vehicle. Several of the windows had been broken out. As the convoy cruised by, deaders inside the building tried to crawl out the broken panes or get to them through the glass still in the other windows, churned into a frenzy by the food passing by.

"This isn't gonna work." Carter's voice came over the radio. *"There's too many of those things in there."*

Dickson picked up his radio. "I want to check out the ER,

first. If it's overrun, we'll try somewhere else."

As he placed the radio back on the dashboard, Nora pointed to the right. "It's in back."

Dickson turned right and headed for the rear of the building. As he expected, carnage had ravaged this part of the hospital as well. Three ambulances sat askew outside the ER entrance, the rear doors open and dried blood covering the interiors and the ground. As he pulled up to the doors, deaders inside the lobby staggered toward the glass walls, banging against them to get out. No way would he risk going in there.

Shifting into park, Dickson climbed out of the Hummer, telling the others to stay in the vehicle. As he walked back to the Chevy, Stratman and Carter joined him.

"What's up?" asked Stratman.

"There's too many deaders in there."

"It's not that bad." Carter stared at the glass walls. "We should be able to take care of them."

Dickson shook his head. "It's too risky. We'll find what we need at one of those docs in a box."

"We won't find the good stuff like morphine," warned Carter.

"I know, but—"

What sounded like three rounds of gunfire interrupted the conversation.

"What the fuck was that?" asked Stratman.

"Cut the engines," ordered Dickson.

Williamson shut down the Chevy. Stratman ran his fingers across his neck, signaling Elaine to do the same, which she did. Dickson yelled to Nora, "Kill the engine."

She leaned out the window. "What?"

"Kill the fucking engine! Now!"

Nora did. Silence fell over the area. A few seconds later, three more gunshots broke the stillness.

"Stay here until I get back." Dickson ran for the Hummer and whipped open the door. "Everyone out."

"What's going on?" asked Joel.

"Do what I fucking tell you!" He crawled in and switched on the engine as the rest jumped out. "Get out of sight until I get back."

A single round fired as Dickson swung the Hummer into a U-turn and headed for the main road. He pulled over against a copse of trees along the driveway, parked, and waited. Only a few minutes elapsed before two vehicles passed by heading south on Route 302. No one spotted him. He waited a few seconds and then inched the Hummer to the edge of the exit, advancing enough so he could keep track of the vehicles and not be spotted. When they disappeared around a bend in the road, he pulled out and followed.

Dickson slowed at the bend and eased out enough to observe the other vehicles, which were a quarter of a mile ahead of him. He waited until they veered right at the next curve before racing down, slowing when he approached it, and staying concealed until they disappeared again. This cat and mouse routine went on for several miles until the two vehicles reached the southern outskirts of town, crossed over the Saco River, and turned right where Route 302 merged with Route 113 West. Dickson raced down to the intersection and inched out, leaning forward against the windshield to spot them.

"Fuck."

Both vehicles were gone. A cross street sat not far away, which meant the drivers had either turned there or had spotted him and were preparing an ambush. He was willing to take that risk. Dickson rushed forward and pulled into the intersection. The cross street to the left extended straight for hundreds of feet. The road to the right, West Side Drive, was the one they had taken earlier when entering town. There were no vehicles on either one. Shit, they must have continued straight. Dickson chased after them. Because this road wound its way through the countryside, he never caught up with them, assuming they must have turned off one of the many dirt roads or driveways he passed.

Luck broke Dickson's way when the road merged again with Route 302. He spotted the two cars a mile to his left rounding a bend in the road and set off in that direction, tracking them the same way he had back in North Conway. However, after several miles he lost them and threw caution to the wind, bringing the Hummer up to almost seventy miles per hour. If he came across them, he'd either turn around or, if confronted, tell them he was on his own and passing through. That never happened. After several minutes, Dickson entered Twin Mountain. He drove through to the opposite side of town without spotting them and pulled over onto the shoulder.

Dickson took the map off the dashboard and studied it. He last spotted the two vehicles at Hart's Location where Route 302 made a sharp turn to the north. He assumed they hadn't traveled this far. If right, that left a twenty-mile stretch of country road they could have turned off, which narrowed his search significantly. If wrong, fuck it, no harm done.

Throwing the map back onto the dashboard, Dickson swung the Hummer around and headed back to the rest of his group.

Chapter Eleven

A LISSA SMILED AS the two vehicles pulled up the driveway to her cabin, happy to finally be home. The recon had been successful, at least as far as gathering information. Only a few deaders remained in the area, so they didn't have to be concerned about being overrun by a swarm of the living dead. On the downside, they now had to worry about that rampaging forest fire on the other side of the mountain. While it posed no immediate threat, unless the area got some rain soon, it could become a problem in the future. She would worry about that later. Right now, she wanted a drink and to pet Archer.

As the four of them parked their vehicles, Miriam rushed out onto the front porch. "I'm so glad you guys are back."

"Is anything wrong?"

"Not at all. Steve picked up someone on the radio."

Alissa and the others ran into cabin. Steve sat at the dining room table listening to a battery-operated radio. He had a notebook in front of him in which he jotted notes. Miriam stood behind him, gently massaging his shoulders.

"What's up?" asked Nathan.

"I got bored reading, so I decided to listen through all the channels on the radio. For shits and giggles." Steve smiled. "When I did, I came across this station."

They all listened. Nothing played.

"I don't hear anything," said Alissa.

"You will. There's a delay between each broadcast." As Miriam spoke, the high-pitched screech of the Emergency Alert

System alarm sounded. She pointed to the radio. "See."

The alarm lasted fifteen seconds and stopped. A moment later, the message began.

This is Colonel Jonathan West of the Maine National Guard, 521ˢᵗ Troop Command. I have recorded this broadcast and am running it on a continuous loop to let any survivors of this crisis know you are not alone. We have established a secure facility in Maine near Islesboro on Warren Island in Penobscot Bay, geocoordinates 44 degrees, 18 minutes, 30 seconds North and 68 degrees, 54 minutes, 12 seconds West. We have established a defensive perimeter, are well armed, and have sufficient supplies to last several months. We are not a refugee camp. I repeat, we are not a refugee camp. We are a fully functional group that is attempting to build a sustainable base of operations to not only protect ourselves from deaders and bandits, but also to gather enough forces to begin taking back this region. Civilians can contact us at 121.5 MHz and any surviving military units at 243.0 MHz. That frequency is manned around the clock. If you are willing to work together in a safe community to preserve what little we have left, you're welcome to join us. If you need assistance getting here, we may be able to help. If you've established your own community, we would love to contact you and figure out a way we could work as a team. In any case, you're not alone.

The broadcast went dead. Thirty seconds later, the EAS alarm interrupted the silence. Steve turned down the volume.

"I ran across that station a little over an hour ago. There are three more stations carrying the same recorded message, but their signals are weak or garbled, so I'm assuming this is either the strongest signal or the one closest to us." Steve picked up the notebook and held it out. "I've copied the text verbatim."

Chris took the notebook, read the transcript, and passed it along to Nathan. "It's good to know there are other communities out there."

Miriam became animated. "Are we going to join up with them?"

"No." Alissa, Nathan, and Chris answered simultaneously.

Miriam appeared crestfallen. "Why not?"

"We don't know if they're legit," answered Nathan. "Suppose we go there and find out it's a labor camp?"

"But the man making the broadcast is a colonel with the National Guard."

Steve reached up and squeezed his wife's hand. "Hon, anyone can claim to be what they want over the radio."

"Besides," added Alissa. "Even if the compound is real, I've seen what happens firsthand when the virus spreads. If one person is bit, that entire compound could be turned within an hour. We're much safer here. We have everything we need."

Miriam turned to her husband for support. He shook his head. "I've got to agree with them. I'd rather be here than in a camp, no matter how secure it might be."

With a sigh, Miriam accepted the inevitable. "Shouldn't we at least let them know we're here?"

"That might not be a bad idea," agreed Chris.

Nathan shook his head. "It's better we keep as low a profile as possible."

"I thought as a cop you'd want to let the authorities know where we are."

"I don't want to deal with some gung-ho asshole who thinks he's in charge and demands the rest of us fall in line, or somebody who wants to rob whoever calls in. Until we know more about this Colonel West and who his group is, our safest bet is keeping a low profile."

Chris turned to Alissa. "Do you agree with him?"

Alissa's mind kept on going back to Hurricane Katrina and how New Orleans fell apart after the storm passed. She remembered the stories of the local police shirking their responsibility to take care of their own families or, in some cases, joining in the looting. Of how the authorities evacuating the city were complete dickheads and forced people to leave their pets behind, something she never would have done to Archer. Of the nightmare stories about what happened in the

Hippodrome, the "safe haven" set up by the authorities for those displaced from their homes. The one image that always stood out, maybe because Paul harped on it all the time, was that the only people in the area who were truly safe were those who banded together to protect one another. She thought they were right then and felt the same way now.

"I do. We have a good arrangement here and I don't want to screw it up." Alissa cut off Chris when he tried to protest. "I think we should check them out to see if they're legit in case we need them in the future but, right now, the fewer people who know about us the better off we are."

"How will we check them out?" asked Kiera. "Are we going to send someone there?"

"No need to." Alissa directed her next question at Steve. "Do you know how to work a ham radio?"

"I haven't used one in ages, but I'm sure it'll come back to me."

"Paul has one stored in the closet. Break it out, set it up, and start listening in and see what you can pick up on local chatter."

"Can do. I assume you want me only to listen in and report back to you."

"Exactly. Don't reach out to anyone under any circumstances."

"Yes, ma'am." Steve gave her a mock salute.

Alissa felt uncomfortable. She didn't like being in charge, but better her than someone else.

Without saying a word, Miriam turned and headed outside to the deck, closing the door hard behind her.

"Did we say something wrong?" Nathan asked in all seriousness.

"PMS," answered Chris.

Steve snickered.

"Screw all of you." Alissa left the table and followed Miriam outside.

Miriam stood by the railing, her elbows resting on top, crying. Alissa approached slowly so as not to startle her.

"Is everything okay?" Alissa mentally kicked herself. If things were okay, Miriam wouldn't be crying.

Miriam wiped the back of her hand under her nose. "Sorry. I shouldn't be so emotional."

"That's fine." Alissa placed a hand on her shoulder. "Do you want to talk?"

Miriam sniffed. "I agree with you and the others. We need to keep a low profile. I just liked the thought of my kids growing up with other kids. Little Stevie has no one his own age to play with and Kiera's becoming a Tomboy."

"For what it's worth, she's a huge help to us."

"Thanks." Miriam forced a smile. "I know that. I always thought that, when Kiera turned fourteen, I'd be preparing her for her first date, not for a search and destroy mission against deaders."

"At least you know Kiera won't let the deaders give her a hickey."

Miriam stared at Alissa, unable to believe what she had heard. Then, as the absurdity of what Alissa said struck her, she chuckled. Alissa joined in. After a few seconds, both women were laughing so loud the men were staring at them through the windows.

Chapter Twelve

"**I** STILL DON'T understand why we're out here," said Nora.

Dickson resisted the urge to slap her. Nora was good in bed, but slow in the head. Truth be told, she didn't do very well at the former. It frustrated the fuck out of him that he already had gone over all this with them.

After giving up the search yesterday for the other vehicles, he had returned to the hospital, picked up the team, and found a service station to rest for the night. Then he explained to them that the people they had encountered were most likely encamped along that twenty-mile stretch of road and they needed to find out where. Last night they understood, or at least claimed to. How fucking difficult was it to comprehend? Parked out in the open at the David Path Trail parking lot was not the time to question what they were doing.

"I told you already. We're trying to figure out where that other group is holing up so we can take over their place."

"I get that," replied Nora. "What I'm saying is, there can't be that many side roads leading into the mountains. Why don't we check them all out until we find these people?"

"That would draw attention to us and make them suspicious."

"Big deal. We find them, take them out, and take over their camp."

Dickson rubbed the bridge of his nose. The bitch gave him a headache.

Carter took over. "Easier said than done. They were driving new vehicles and one of them, probably all four of them, had semi-automatic weapons."

"So do we," protested Nora. "And there's eight of us versus four of them."

"You don't get it, do you? We can't go barging in. We have no idea where they are, how many there are, what they have in the way of weapons. Plus, they have the advantage of being on the defense. If we try it your way, the chances are fifty-fifty we'll get our asses handed to us. Do you understand now?"

"Yes." Nora spat the word with as much venom as embarrassment.

"What exactly are we looking for?" asked Rebecca.

Dickson picked up the briefing. "Anything that narrows down where they are. Smoke from a fire, people walking along hiking trails, barking dogs, anything that indicates people. Once we find them, Carter and I will check them out and we can go from there."

"What if they run into us?" Stratman asked the others. "Do we fight them? Run?"

"Ignore them unless they engage you. If they do, tell them you're passing through and are taking a break. See if you can get info out of them without sounding suspicious."

"And radio the rest of us the minute they leave so we can take cover," added Carter.

"What are we going to do about her?" Stratman motioned to the Chevy where Connie sat in the front seat. Dickson had left Diana and Brian back at the service station handcuffed to a radiator and took the girl along as collateral, warning Diana what they would do to Connie if she ran off.

"Warn her what'll happen to her mother and brother if she opens her mouth."

Stratman nodded and smiled.

"Are we all clear on what we're supposed to do?" Dickson glared at Nora.

Everyone responded in the affirmative.

"Good. Let's go."

Elaine and Williamson stayed at the Davis Path Trail parking lot with the cargo van. Joel stayed with them so they could keep an eye on him. Stratman took Rebecca to act as Connie's mother and drove the Chevy to the far end of the zone, parking between Twin Mountains and the Omni Mount Washington Resort. Dickson, Carter, and Nora chose a scenic overlook for Mount Washington halfway between them. Once in place, the teams waited.

And waited.

And waited.

More than four hours passed and the only sounds Dickson heard were birds chirping and Nora bitching. He lost count of how many cigarettes he had burned through, how many bottles of water he had drank, and how many times he had peed.

Nora strolled through the park, reading the historical plaques about Mount Washington and the surrounding peaks for the umpteenth time, then raced back to the Hummer. She grabbed a bunch of napkins from the glove compartment and headed for the woods.

"Be right back. I gotta take a dump."

Dickson waited until she stepped out of earshot. "If we're lucky she'll be eaten by a deader or a bear."

Carter chuckled. "Nice way to talk about your girlfriend."

"She's a fucking pain in the ass. You know it as well as I do."

"Admit it. You have a thing for the new bitch Rebecca."

"Why not. She's hot, she's of use around here, and—"

"She's not Nora."

"Exactly." Dickson laughed.

"Williamson likes Nora. Let him have her."

"I like the kid too much to do that to him." Dickson sighed. "Once we take over this new place and settle down, there'll be some changes—"

A familiar sound broke the stillness around them, sending

birds scattering from the nearby trees.

"Is that what I think it is?" asked Carter.

"It is. It's gunfire." Dickson opened the driver's door to the Humvee and picked up the radio off the dashboard. "We found what we're looking for."

Chapter Thirteen

A S THEY HAD on previous days, Nathan took Kiera to their makeshift shooting range. Alissa and Miriam tagged along, ostensibly to engage in target practice although, in truth, they joined for a reason to get out of the cabin. Miriam hated the idea of bringing her daughter along when they left the compound, but they had no choice. They were short of personnel. Nathan wanted Kiera to become comfortable with weapons, which she had, and to be proficient in their use.

Today Nathan trained Kiera on the FAL battle rifle. As he explained how it functioned and taught her how to use it, the two women stepped over to the end of the range and sat on a fallen tree, resting their Mossbergs beside them.

"I know it's not easy for you," said Alissa.

"The whole end of the world thing?"

"No. Letting Kiera learn how to use firearms."

"I still hate the idea of it. But Kiera is old enough to handle a weapon and she needs to learn how to defend herself if she's going to survive. I've gotten use to that. I hate to think this will be the rest of her life. And Stevie's." Miriam covered her eyes with her hands as the tears flowed.

Alissa wrapped an arm around Miriam and pulled her in. "It's okay. Let it out."

"It's not okay. Nothing will ever be okay again. You, me, Steve, Nathan. We'll adapt. I can deal with that. What about my kids? Everything they've known is gone. No schools. No books. No movies. No games. How are they going to get an education? How are they going to learn to socialize? How are they going to date, fall in love, marry, and have families of their own? Is this their future? Hunting for deaders, foraging for food, scavenging for supplies? Maybe in the long run they'd have been better off if... if...."

"You don't mean that."

"No, I don't." Miriam sniffed and wiped her nose and eyes. "Everything seems so bleak right now."

"It is. But look on the positive side."

Miriam chuckled. "Now you sound like a mother."

"I'm serious. Not only are you and your family alive, you're safe and in a secure location. Sure, things suck now. This outbreak won't last forever. Someday things will return to normal. Well, at least to a life where we can go back to doing what we used to without having to worry about deaders."

"Do you really believe that?"

"I have to otherwise I'd go insane. If I thought that everything I had to do to make it here, all the people I had to leave behind, merely bought me a few extras months before the entire world came to an end, I'd probably use the shotgun on myself."

The comment stunned Miriam. "I'm surprised to hear you talk like this."

"It's true. There must be people still alive out there, good people like us who are laying low. Once we catch our breath and reorganize, we'll take back the world from the living dead and rebuild society."

Miriam leaned over and hugged Alissa.

"Gross!" Of course, the cry came from Kiera.

"Are you two done for the day?" Alissa asked.

"Yup. Uncle Nate says I'm becoming a crack shot, whatever that means."

Nathan patted her on the shoulder. "Since you're getting so good at this, why don't you take point and lead us back to the cabin?"

Kiera took off into the woods with Nathan close behind. Miriam and Alissa pushed themselves off the log and grabbed their shotguns. Miriam reached out and gave Alissa's hand a friendly squeeze.

"Thanks. You're a good friend."

The two women headed back to the cabin.

"WHAT DO YOU think?" whispered Carter. "Do you want to take them?"

Dickson and Carter watched the group from behind a mid-sized boulder on a ledge above the shooting range. After hearing the gun shots yesterday, they had made their way into the woods searching for the source, but whoever fired had stopped before Dickon and Carter could find them. Both men walked the area for hours until they stumbled upon a clearing overlooking a ridge and filled with spent shell casings. Noting the location, they backtracked to the Hummer, rounded up the others, and returned to the service station for the night. This morning, he and Carter made sure they got here early and found a secure place to wait for the shooters. They had been here a while, freezing off their asses even though the temperature hovered in the mid-forties. As expected, the shooters—a man, two women, and a teenage girl—showed up and began target practice. At least, the teenager did. The women sat by themselves chatting. Dickson couldn't help but notice the tits on the brunette.

"Hey." Carter tapped Dickson's arm. "What do you want to do?"

"Nothing yet."

"We can take them by surprise."

"Too risky. If they fight back, those shotguns could do a number on us."

Carter huffed. "Are we giving up the idea of taking their

place?"

"No. I want to follow them and get a better feel for it. We need to know how many are there and what their defenses are like. This is probably our only chance of sitting out this fucking apocalypse in style and I don't want to... get down."

The shooters finished target practice and headed back into the woods. Dickson and Carter waited until they out of sight before setting off after them.

Chapter Fourteen

DICKSON HAD GATHERED the rest of the team during dinner to discuss his plans for tomorrow, and to rally the troops, as he liked to say. Stratman listened because he had to. He and Dickson had devised the plan earlier that afternoon, so he knew what would go down better than everyone else. And Stratman knew Dickson's pep talks by heart. Shit, he had been listening to them since high school when Dickson would entice the others to get into trouble with him. Dickson stressed several times that, if each of them did what they were assigned, by this time tomorrow night they would be sleeping in comfortable beds, be well stocked, and would more than likely have better food to eat. He even mentioned that there would be some new pussy to try out, although he intended the suggestion to entice Williamson and Carter more than anyone else. Those two had already drank the Kool-Aid and believed whatever line of shit Dickson fed them.

Although Stratman would never admit it, not even to Dickson, he had a bad vibe about tomorrow. They needed to find a decent place to hunker down and get off the road, and this cabin seemed to provide an ideal opportunity. Not knowing what their defenses were like, how many people lived there, and what type of weapons they carried, the best plan was to lure out these people and capture them rather than a frontal attack that could get most of them killed. Under the circumstances, the plan he and Dickson had devised appeared the most promising.

However, he didn't believe they could pull it off with this bunch.

The most reliable in the group were Carter, Williamson, and Elaine. Carter was tough, could hold his own, and had street smarts. Just as important, he followed orders and knew his place. The same could be said about Elaine. Williamson... well, he did what Dickson told him to and caused no problems. If Williamson stayed with him or Carter or Elaine, he'd be fine. If left by himself, Stratman doubted the kid would survive for long.

Although reliable and loyal, Nora didn't have the same experience as the others. Dickson had taken her as his girl-friend. Only Stratman knew that was a farce. Dickson had not been able to get it up for two years due to a testosterone imbalance or some such medical bullshit. Not that it mattered. It boiled down to Dickson's relationship with Nora being a token to make him seem tough in the eyes of the others. Nora played the part to be spared from being a plaything for the rest of them and because she knew what would happen if she revealed the truth.

Joel was fucking useless. His only contribution lay in being such a coward he'd do whatever they told him. Ironically, his girlfriend Rebecca had proven more of an asset. Stratman laughed to himself. He meant former girlfriend. The night Joel let the others have their way with her killed whatever relation-ship they might have had. Rebecca knew if she didn't want to spend the rest of her life in the Chevy with Diana and the brats, she needed to make herself useful. So far, she had done a good job.

Stratman had not given much thought to Diana and the kids. He had supported the idea of bringing them along to use as bait and to send into stores for supplies so none of them got hurt. Dickson made them ride in the bed of the pick-up, his way of showing them all who ran the show. Once they were all set up in the cabin and didn't need the family anymore, he hated to think what would become of them.

Dickson would be the most unpredictable factor. The two of them had been best friends since high school. Dickson had been a bit of asshole back then, bullying weaker kids, mouthing off to teachers, skipping class. After graduation, they had done a lot of shit that, if they were caught, probably would have landed them in jail or at least probation. Fortunately, they both knew when they were about to step over the line and had enough common sense to pull back.

Well, except for that one time in Albany when Dickson let his anger get the better of him. Jesus, that almost became a clusterfuck. They were in town, bar hopping with fake IDs, when some assfuck banged into Dickson's car and took off. Dickson tracked him down and forced him off the road, screaming at the driver about what he had done and demanding he pay to fix it. The altercation turned into a fight that ended with Dickson almost bashing in the driver's head. Only the timely arrival of the cops prevented Dickson from killing the driver. They both would have wound up in jail except for the fact that the driver had hit and run, thrown the first punch, and happened to be a wanted sex offender who had skipped bail. The event had scared the shit out of Dickson and, for a while, he calmed down. However, with the world having gone to Hell, that uncontrolled friend from high school reared its ugly head.

Dickson finished his pep talk. "Any questions?"

Stratman doubted they would ask, even if they did.

"Then get some sleep. We have a big day ahead of us." Dickson motioned for Stratman to walk with him.

"Is everything set for tomorrow?"

Stratman nodded. "Everyone checked their vehicles and their weapons."

"Good job. With luck, we'll finally be able to settle down."

"That would be nice."

"Excuse me." Rebecca approached cautiously, not wanting

to piss off Dickson.

"What?"

"What about the leftover food? Can I give it to Diana and her kids?"

Dickson thought for a moment. "Why not. After tomorrow night, we'll have more than enough."

"Thank you."

As Rebecca left, Stratman spoke softly no one else could hear. "Have you considered what you're going to do with Diana and the kids once we take over the cabin?"

"I hadn't really thought about it." Dickson mulled over the thought. "Probably let them go. The little girl is of no use to us and the teenager has a broken arm."

"What about the people in the cabin?"

"They'll get a choice. They're welcome to stay, if they do what we tell them. Someone is going to have go into buildings and get supplies, especially after we ditch the bitch and her kids."

"If there's a lot of them?" asked Stratman.

"We'll keep the most pliable ones and eliminate the others." Dickson paused and stared coldly at Stratman. "Do you have a problem with that?"

"No," Stratman lied.

"Then why did you ask?"

"If they fight back, I wanted to know if we needed them alive or whether they're expendable."

"They're all expendable." Dickson smirked and walked away.

Stratman watched him go and shook his head. He felt no better about tomorrow.

Chapter Fifteen

"**N**O WAY." KIERA shook her head violently. "Stay away from me."

"For God's sake," sighed Miriam. "All I'm asking is to cut your hair. You look like an anime character."

"That's how I like it."

"Come on, Kiera." Little Stevie lifted his head as his mother trimmed the back. Miriam pushed his head down. "If I have to do it, you do."

"You're a kid."

"So are you." Miriam chastised Kiera in her best mom voice.

"I like it this way." Kiera unconsciously pushed several long strands off her face and behind her ear.

Miriam grinned. "Shake your head."

Kiera moved it an inch from side to side.

"Really shake it."

Kiera did so. When she finished, hair covered her eyes. She quickly pushed it away from her face.

"That settles it. You're getting a haircut."

"Yay!" Little Stevie raised his head to cheer his sister having to share his misery. Miriam pushed his head down again.

Alissa and Nathan entered after doing a check of the perimeter.

Kiera waved her arms dramatically. "You gotta help me."

"What now?" joked Nathan.

"Mom wants to give me a haircut."

"You need one. You remind me of Moe Howard."

"Who?" Kiera asked.

Nathan laughed. "Never mind."

"Alissa," Kiera pleaded. "You have to help me."

"Sorry, kid. You're on your own."

"Do you want me to look like Little Stevie?"

"I doubt your mother would give you a crew cut." Alissa glanced over at Miriam. "Would you?"

"Of course not. My daughter is practicing for the Academy Award."

Kiera rolled her eyes. "My mother can't cut hair. I'll look like I had a bowl on my head."

Alissa circled around Little Stevie. "There's nothing wrong with his haircut."

"Don't listen to her." Miriam put down the scissors. "I learned to cut hair after high school. I opened my own shop but had to give it up."

"Why?"

Miriam brushed the loose hair off Little Stevie's shoulders. When finished, he stood up and shook himself off. "It became too expensive between rent and insurance. I was barely breaking even. I gave it up after I had Little Stevie to spend more time with the kids, but I can still give a good haircut."

"Depending on how well you do on Kiera, I may ask for one myself."

"Great." Kiera moved over to the table. "I'm a friggin' guinea pig."

Miriam gently cuffed her daughter on the side of her head. "Language, young lady."

Kiera plopped into the chair, knowing when she had lost.

From outside the cabin, an unfamiliar voice yelled, "Hello? Is anyone there?"

Nathan grabbed his FAL and headed for the door. Kiera joined him, staying low and gazing out the corner of the window, ready to use the other FAL if necessary. A woman walked up the driveway, approaching the cabin cautiously, moving forward a few steps and stopping. She appeared haggard, her long red hair scraggly and unwashed, her face and loose-fitting clothes caked with a layer of dirt. The woman had a genuine expression of fear on her face.

"Hello? Is anyone there?"

Nathan raised the window to the left of the door. "That's close enough. What do you want?"

The woman stopped and backed up. "My boyfriend is sick and I need help."

"Stay where you are." Nathan closed the window and whispered to Kiera. "Keep an eye on her."

"Gotcha."

Nathan turned to Miriam. "Where's Steve?"

"Upstairs taking a nap."

"Join him. Take Little Stevie with you. Don't come down until I tell you to."

As Miriam ushered her son upstairs, Nathan returned to the window and raised it again. Alissa joined him, clutching the Mossberg.

"Raise your hands and turn around."

"What?"

"You heard me. Raise your arms and turn around."

The woman obeyed.

"Approach slowly and stop at the bottom of the stairs," Nathan ordered.

"Are you going to help me?"

"Just do as you're told."

As the woman came closer, Nathan snapped his fingers to get Kiera's attention. "Take your gun and go upstairs with your mother."

Kiera's spirits deflated. "Because I'm a kid?"

"I don't want her knowing how many of us are here. If this goes south, you're my back up. You okay with that?"

"Of course." Kiera ran across the living room and up the

stairs. As she did, she heard the front door open and Nathan say, "What's your name?"

"Nora."

"Nora, come on in, but don't try anything stupid."

THE ALARM ON Dickson's watch sounded. He shut it off and double checked the clock inside the van. Thirty minutes had passed since Nora had left the Hummer in the driveway and walked up to the cabin.

"That means she's in."

"What if they shot her?" asked Stratman.

Dickson shrugged. "We would have heard it."

A few minutes passed. Dickson patted the dashboard. "Let's go back to town and set up the ambush."

Chapter Sixteen

N ORA SAT AT the dining room table, her back to the rest of the cabin, looking as nervous as she did haggard. Alissa sat opposite her, studying the woman and trying to imagine what nightmares she must have gone through. Nathan stood slightly behind Nora and to her left, his eyes never once leaving the woman.

"Can I get you anything to drink?" Alissa asked.

"A cup of coffee would be nice. Milk and sugar, if you have it."

"We don't have milk."

"That's okay."

Alissa stood, but Nathan headed for the kitchen. "I'll make it."

"Why do you need our help?" asked Alissa.

"It's my boyfriend, Richie. We holed up in one of the hotels in North Conway. We were going through the rooms, clearing the place of deaders and looking for anything we could use, when he slipped and fell down some stairs. He broke his ankle. He's in a lot pain. I came looking for help."

Nathan came out of the kitchen holding a mug of coffee that he placed on the table in front of Nora. "Here you go."

"Thanks." Nora took a sip and winced. "It tastes weird."

"Sorry about that. We're out of sugar so I used a liquid sweetener. Did I put in too much?"

"It'll be fine." Nora took a long sip.

"I'll get you something to eat." Alissa went into the kitchen for some crackers. She noticed that Nathan had removed the bottle of Stolichnaya from the freezer. It sat by the coffee maker, the top resting on the counter. She placed a dozen crackers on a plate and took them back to the dining room.

"Thank you." Nora pulled the plate towards her and shoved a cracker into her mouth.

"Which hotel did you hole up in?" asked Nathan.

"I don't remember the name. It's in the center of North Conway. I know how to get there."

"How long ago did the two of you arrive in town?"

"Two days."

"What about the deaders?"

"There were a few, but they ignored us. They seemed more interested in heading north." Nora paused. "Why?"

"I want to get an idea of what we're up against." Nathan moved to her left. "How come you didn't bring Ricky with you?"

"He's too big for me to carry."

"Rickey's not immobile if it's only his ankle," said Nathan. "Couldn't he limp?"

Nora turned her attention to Alissa. "Can you help?"

"I'm a nurse. I can help."

"Do you have everything you need to fix him up?"

Nathan cut Alissa off before she could answer. "We're barely managing."

"We should get going," pleaded Nora. "Before the deaders find him."

"I thought you said there were no deaders in town."

"There aren't." Nora responded quickly, then thought for a moment. "But there are some of those things inside the hotel."

"I thought they were locked in their rooms?"

"They could get out."

Nathan paused. "How did you find us? We're a long way from North Conway."

"It took me a while. There's no one in town so I drove

through the residential areas looking for help. Everyone's dead or gone. I found myself on Route 302 checking out every driveway I came across until I found you. I've been driving around for hours."

Nathan entered the kitchen and came out a moment later with a map of North Conway. He placed it in front of Nora. "Which hotel is he trapped in?"

"I'm not sure."

"Please find it."

As Nora studied the map, Nathan gestured for Alissa to join him in the kitchen.

"You know she's setting us up," he whispered.

"Her story checks out."

"Some of it checks out. She can't even remember her boy-friend's name."

"What do you mean?"

"She called him Richie. When I referred to him as Rickey, she didn't correct me."

Alissa rolled her eyes. "You're being paranoid. She's nervous, that's all."

"I know when someone's lying to me."

"We can't leave him there."

"Are you certain you're not trying to soothe your conscience about the people you left behind in Boston?"

Alissa bristled but maintained her calm. "You stay here if you want. I'm going to help."

Nathan sighed. "I'm not letting you go alone. But if you get me killed, I'm not speaking to you again."

Without waiting for a response, Nathan took the radio off the counter and slid it into his pocket, then exited the kitchen.

"Have you figured out which hotel it is?"

"Yes." Nora pointed to the map. "The Grand Hotel."

"Good. We'll help you. Give me a few minutes to gather our gear."

"Thank you." Nora turned to Alissa as she entered the

dining room. "Thank you, both."

Nathan went out onto the deck and moved to the far corner. He removed the radio from his pocket and spoke to
someone for several minutes, then came back inside and went
upstairs. Five minutes later he came back down holding the
FAL and Mossberg and three pistols, a Colt .45 in its holster
which he strapped around his waist and the two 10mm Smith
and Wesson revolvers. Alissa watched him insert one of the
revolvers between the small of his back and his pants, covering
it with his leather jacket. He stepped over to the table and
placed the other one in front of Nora.

"What's this for?" she asked.

"In case we run into any trouble. Now finish your coffee."

Alissa mouthed the words thank you to Nathan. He ignored
her.

As Nora drank down the last of the coffee, Nathan asked,
"Where's your vehicle?"

"I left it around the bend in the driveway."

"What is it?"

"A Hummer."

"Excellent. We'll take that."

Ten minutes later, the three of them climbed into the
Hummer, with Nathan driving, and headed into North
Conway.

WHAT NO ONE realized at the time was that the winds from the
north had picked up a day ago and driven the forest fire out of
the gulley into the northern part of North Conway. Once it
reached buildings, the lack of rain allowed the conflagration to
proliferate rapidly. Within the past few hours, flames overran
the upper three quarters of the city and spread to within a
hundred yards of the Grand Hotel. To the east of the hotel,
where nothing but woods existed, the fire had moved farther

south and already had moved past the structure, threatening to trap anyone still inside the city.

To make matters worse, the flames, smoke, and roar could be seen and heard for miles. Every deader within a twenty-mile radius now converged on the city, including those from Conway, the surrounding towns, and those wandering the nearby forests. As Alissa, Nathan, and Nora entered the city from the south, three hundred deaders closed in behind them, threatening to close off the city in a pincer move.

Chapter Seventeen

A WALL OF flames spread across North Conway as the Hummer moved along the main road.

"Jesus, I hope we're not too late." It was the first honest expression Nora had uttered since arriving at the cabin.

"We don't have much time," said Nathan. "We'll get in, get your boyfriend, and get out before we're all dead."

"Sure."

The hesitation in Nora's voice did not register with Alissa, her full attention drawn to the conflagration bearing down on them. This terrified her more than Boston. Alissa tamped down the frightened woman in her and let the nurse take over. She started planning how they would rescue Nora's boyfriend, bring him back to the Hummer, and haul their asses out before they burned alive.

Nora pointed to a road off to the right. "The hotel is down there."

Nathan turned and headed into Settler's Green Village, an outdoor mall composed of outlet stores. The Grand Hotel was located behind the village, though difficult to see through the pall of black smoke that hung over the area. The woods behind the hotel already burned furiously. Embers from the fire floated over the area, covering everything in a layer of ash, forcing Nathan to switch on the windshield wipers. As they took the access road around the village and approached the hotel, Alissa noticed a dozen spots on the roof smoldering. The entire area would be an inferno within minutes.

FROM HIS PERCH on top of Levi's Outlet Store on the left side of the access road, Stratman watched the Hummer enter the plaza and pass beneath him. He aimed his Howa bolt-action hunting rifle on the vehicle, studying the interior through the scope. He had a clear line of sight to the hotel entrance. Stratman picked up his radio.

"Boss, they're here."

"*How many?*"

"Just Nora, a man, and a woman. They're in the Hummer."

"*Fuck. There should be at least two more.*"

"They probably stayed behind to keep an eye on the cabin."

"*We'll deal with them later. Stay alert in case they arrive as back up.*"

"Roger that. Elaine, did you hear the boss?"

"*I did,*" Elaine answered from her position on top of Banana Republic across the street from Levi's.

"*Same here.*" The response came from Williamson, who stayed with the van parked behind Levi's, ready to get them all away quickly if things went wrong. "*Let's hurry it up. That fire is getting too fucking close.*"

"Calm down. The boss knows what he's doing." Stratman waited a moment. "Asshole, are you there?"

JOEL AND REBECCA stood outside the Chevy parked behind the hotel. The fire had reached the access road on the other side of the parking lot that paralleled the forest. The intense heat and embers caused the grass and bushes on islands scattered around the parking lot to catch fire, bringing the danger that much closer.

"*Hey, asshole. Can you fucking hear me?*"

Joel keyed the radio.

"I'm here."

"*Did you here any of that? We're about to set the trap.*"

"I heard."

"*Hang tight until I tell you to move.*"

Rebecca took the radio from Joel. "Can we move our position? The fire is getting close."

"*If you move now, you could give us away.*"

"We're in danger here."

"*I don't give a shit. Asshole, are you there?*"

Joel ripped the radio away from Rebecca, glaring at her. "I'm here."

"*If you break ranks the boss will hold you responsible. You know what that means.*"

Joel gulped. "I do."

"*Then sit tight until you hear from me.*"

"Sure thing."

From inside the Chevy's bed, Diana yelled. "Please let us out. We won't cause trouble."

"No," snapped Joel.

"We're burning up in here."

"Fuck off." He raised his Remington Model 870 shotgun and aimed it at the canopy.

"Joel," urged Rebecca. "Lower the shotgun."

"No way. I'm not getting my ass kicked for them."

"You had no problem letting me be raped, though."

Joel lowered the Remington and gazed into her eyes. "I'm sorry about that."

Rebecca didn't buy it. "Let them out so they can stand around in the air. If they try anything, you have the shotgun."

"No. Now all of you, shut the fuck up."

Joel turned away, unable to make eye contact with Rebecca.

CHRIS DROVE DOWN Route 302, keeping a watchful eye on his surroundings, concerned about both the fire closing in around them and the possibility of an ambush. Nathan had called thirty minutes ago and informed him about Nora arriving at the cabin, the bullshit story she told, and Alissa insisting they go save this so-called boyfriend. Nathan needed back up in case there were more of these assholes than he could handle. Chris showed up at the cabin ten minutes later, after the others had departed, to pick up Miriam and Kiera and arm himself with the Mk14 sniper rifle. Once certain Steve could defend the cabin if necessary, he loaded the women in the Ram and headed for North Conway.

"The road to the hotel is a few hundred feet ahead of us," said Kiera from the backseat. She held the map open in front of her, resting it on the FAL battle rifle that lay across her lap.

Chris pulled the Ram into the parking lot of a family restaurant not far from the entrance to Settler's Green Village. A line of trees ran between him and the outlet stores and hotel, preventing them from being seen. He shifted into park and turned off the engine.

"What now?" asked Kiera.

"We wait to hear from Nathan that everything is okay and help him get Nora and her boyfriend to safety or, if the shit hits the fan, we save them in the nick of time."

"I don't like this." Miriam sat up front, the Mossberg between her legs and pointed toward the floorboard. "We never should have involved Kiera."

"Mom!"

Chris held up his hand to stop the argument. "We have to assume these people are after the cabin. If we don't stop them here, then we fight it out back home where Little Stevie is. Trust me, this is the best way."

NORA POINTED TO the front entrance of the Grand Hotel. "He's in there."

Nathan pulled the Hummer under the sheltered carport, shut off the engine, and pocketed the keys. He stepped out and wrapped the strap of his FAL around his neck, holding it in the high-ready position. The two women joined him. He raised a hand to stop them and stepped into the lobby, scanning it from one end to the other.

"All clear. Let's hurry before we get trapped in here."

Nora entered and crossed over to the admission's desk, circling behind the counter. "I left Richie in the office where he'd be safe."

Nora opened the office door and stepped aside, allowing Alissa to enter. A man sat on the desk whom Alissa assumed was Richie. His legs dangled over the side. As Nathan stepped up beside Alissa, the man slid off the desk onto both feet, showing no signs of pain, and raised a Colt 1911, pointing it at Nathan. Nora moved up behind Nathan and placed the barrel of the Smith and Wesson against the back of his head.

"Don't be a hero and you'll live."

Nathan released his grip on the FAL and raised his hands.

Alissa started to raise the Mossberg when a man in a red beard stepped out from behind the open door and placed the barrel of an AK-47 against her left temple. "I wouldn't do that."

Alissa hesitated and looked to Nathan for guidance. He nodded for her to comply. She moved her right hand from the trigger and held it out to the side.

"Smart move, honey." The man took the shotgun from Alissa with his left hand and slung it over his shoulder. Switching his position to the right, he pulled the Glock from her holster and slid it behind his back, then moved back. Glancing over her shoulder, she noticed the semi-automatic aimed at her back.

Nora had already taken Nathan's FAL from around his neck, placing it around her own, and pulled his Colt from the holster, holding it in her left hand.

Nathan leaned his head to one side and whispered in a voice loud enough for everyone to hear. "I told you the bitch couldn't be trusted."

"Shut up, asshole." Nora jammed the Smith and Wesson against his head and pushed, trying to intimidate him.

"Who many others were at the cabin?" asked Dickson.

"None that I could see."

Dickson leaned back against the edge of the desk. "So, you're keeping the other two hidden. I'd say you're clever but you walked into this. That's neither here nor there. To get to the point, my people need a safe place to stay and supplies to keep us going, and you have what we want. The deal is simple. You share what you have with us and we'll let you stay if you don't cause trouble. Otherwise, we take it from you anyway and leave you for the deaders. What's your answer?"

Nathan smiled. "Fuck you to Hell, and this cunt you rode in on."

"I like a man who stands by his convictions, as long as they're my convictions." Dickson looked at Nora. "Shoot him."

"My pleasure." Nora sneered. "Good riddance, dickless."

Nora leveled the Smith and Wesson at Nathan's head and pulled the trigger.

Chapter Eighteen

T HE HAMMER STRUCK the chamber.

Nothing happened.

Nathan spun to his left, smashing his left elbow into Nora's face. Her jaw cracked with a loud snap. Blood and broken teeth flew across the office. He continued circling around, grabbing Nora by the hair with his left hand and shoving the woman in front of him as a shield. With his right, Nathan pulled his 10mm Smith and Wesson from under his leather jacket, aimed it at Dickson, and fired two rounds.

Dickson rolled backwards across the desk and dropped behind it as the rounds slammed into the surface where he had been leaning. Splinters of wood blasted out from the chair opening, peppering his face. One struck him in the left eye, blurring his vison.

Rage surged inside Alissa. She had placed her faith in Nora, had trusted her training as a first responder rather than her gut instinct, and these assholes responded by trying to execute them. Fuck being a care giver.

When Carter stepped in front of Alissa and switched his aim to Nathan, she clutched the stock and barrel of the AK-47, pushing his aim to the right as he fired. The rounds punched into the desk under which Dickson cowered. Alissa placed the heel of her right boot on his right shin, dug it in, and drove it down. He screamed as the rubber ripped open the skin and tore up the muscles. Alissa yanked the weapon out of his hand and smashed him three times in the face with the stock, shattering his front teeth and breaking his nose. Carter dropped to his knees. Blood poured down his face. Alissa smashed the stock against his temple, knocking him to the floor where he lay semi-conscious. She swung the weapon over her shoulder, yanked the Mossberg off his arm, and removed her Glock from his pants. Alissa aimed the Mossberg at Carter's head.

With the gunfire temporarily halted, Dickson popped up from behind the desk and fired his Colt 1911 three times at Nathan. All three rounds impacted against Nora's chest, killing her instantly. She went limp in Nathan's hand.

Alissa spun around and fired the Mossberg at Carter but her aim was off. The round hit the desktop, scattering the buckshot. Several hit Dickson in the chest and arms. He cried out and dropped behind the desk.

Nathan dragged Nora's corpse in front of him as he moved toward the lobby.

"Let's go."

Alissa ran to the door, keeping the Mossberg trained on the desk. Once they both reached the door, Nathan let Nora drop to the floor, retrieved his weapons and her 10mm Smith and Wesson, and ran for the entrance. Alissa fired two more rounds into the desk and followed, keeping her shotgun trained on the office. They climbed into the Hummer. Nathan started the engine as Alissa grabbed the radio.

"It's a trap."

"*Are you and Nathan okay?*"

"Yes. We're on our way to you. Get ready to roll."

"*YES. WE'RE ON our way to you. Get ready to roll.*"

"You heard the lady." Chris started the Ram. "Be ready to provide cover."

Miriam and Kiera stepped outside and crouched behind the opened doors, using them as cover.

DICKSON HEARD THE Hummer's engine. He popped up from behind the desk and fired at the doorway in case one of the assholes had stayed behind to provide cover. The bullets harmlessly imbedded in the wall.

"Fuck!"

Across the office, Carter moaned as he struggled to stand. Blood flowed from his shin, his broken nose, and a gash along the side of his head. He rolled onto his hands and knees, spitting out fragments of broken teeth.

"You let that bitch get the better of you. And she stole your weapons."

"Sorry, boss."

Dickson kicked the desk, breaking the side paneling. Finding the radio laying on the floor, he picked it up and raced into the lobby, almost tripping over Nora's body. The assholes had taken her weapons as well. He keyed the radio.

"Those motherfuckers are trying to escape. Don't let them get off this compound. Capture them alive if possible. I want to deal with them myself."

WEAPONS FIRING ECHOED from inside the hotel. Joel and Rebecca looked at each other in confusion.

"Were those gunshots?" asked Joel.

"Sounds like it." Rebecca couldn't even begin to imagine what nightmare those who had been suckered into the hotel were going through.

"What should we—"

"Those motherfuckers are trying to escape. Don't let them get off this compound. Capture them alive if possible. I want to deal with them myself."

Joel keyed the radio. "We'll be right there."

He turned to Rebecca. "Let's move. The boss is in—"

Rebecca punched Joel in the face. The blow merely stunned him. She punched him three more times until he dropped to the ground unconscious. She picked up the Remington and approached the Chevy. Stepping to the side, Rebecca shot off the locked handle to the cap, raised the lid, and lowered the tailgate.

In the back, Diana hugged her kids. "Please don't hurt us."

"We're getting out of here."

"What's going on?"

"I have no idea. But if we don't move now, we'll be stuck here until Dickson decides to kill us." Rebecca reached inside and offered her hand.

Connie took it and Rebecca helped her out of the bed. Diana hesitated.

"It's now or never."

Diana assisted her son across the bed, Brian wincing the entire time. Rebecca lowered him off the tailgate.

"Are you okay?"

"I've been better," he groaned.

Diana exited the Chevy. "Where do we go?"

Rebecca glanced around. The fire extended south of the hotel, and the lawn and shrubs around the parking lot burned. Beyond the parking lot, a road ran south that seemed relatively safe.

"We'll go that way. Now hurry."

"THOSE MOTHERFUCKERS ARE trying to escape. Don't let them get off this compound. Capture them alive if possible. I want to deal with them myself."

Through the haze, Stratman saw white exhaust coming from the tailpipe of the Hummer parked under the sheltered entrance to the motel. Without wasting time to respond to Dickson, he aimed the hunting rifle. He had no clear view inside the vehicle, so he waited, lining up his shot to take out the driver the moment he drove away.

ELAINE HAD NO line of sight from her position atop Banana Republic. She could only see the second story of the Grand Hotel over the rooftops of the outlet stores.

Moving over to the access hatch in the roof, she climbed down to the main floor and made her way outside.

DICKSON RUSHED ACROSS the lobby, firing through the plate glass doors and windows at the Hummer. He succeeded only in shattering the panes, warning them of the approaching danger.

"HE'S COMING," WARNED Alissa as she pumped two more rounds into the lobby, causing Dickson and Carter to dive out of the line of fire.

Nathan shifted into drive and pushed his foot on the accelerator. The Hummer shot out from beneath the sheltered driveway. The left rear window blew out, showering them in glass. Nathan paid no attention, assuming the bullet had come from inside the hotel. Turning left, he crossed the island, bounced into the parking lot, and headed for Route 302, an escape that took him directly in front of the Levi's store.

"SHIT!"

The Hummer had pulled away from the hotel faster than Stratman had anticipated and his first shot missed the driver, blowing out the rear window instead. He chambered a second round and lined up another shot, aiming ahead of the vehicle. At the last second, the Hummer turned and raced toward him, trying to escape the outlet mall.

Stratman adjusted his aim onto the driver.

"*Sayonara*, you son of a bitch."

Stratman squeezed the trigger.

A BULLET STRUCK the Hummer's windshield, spider-webbing the glass and lodging into the driver's headrest, missing Nathan by inches. Stopping would make them sitting ducks, so Nathan pressed his foot on the accelerator and spun the Hummer into a U-turn. Another shot rang out, and a second later the back window exploded, showering them in glass. Nathan raced for the rear of the hotel, swerving to throw off the sniper's aim.

As they passed by the hotel entrance, Alissa saw movement on her right. Dickson rushed out of the hotel and ran across the parking lot, raising his Colt. She had time to yell only one word.

"Duck!"

DICKSON STOOD AT the lobby entrance, watching the assholes steal his Hummer. Carter hobbled up alongside him.

"Fucking son of a bitch!" Dickson kicked the metal ashtray stand by the door, sending it flying down the driveway.

A gunshot rang out and the Hummer's windshield cracked.

Dickson did a fist pump. "Stratman nailed the motherfucker."

The Hummer spun around and darted across the parking lot, heading for the rear of the hotel, and passing within thirty feet of them. Dickson ran toward them, firing his revolver as it passed, each round punching into the metal with no effect. He stopped, calculated the speed and direction of the vehicle, and waited for it to turn. When it veered right to go behind the hotel, the cunt's head came into view. He led the Hummer and pulled the trigger.

Click.

Only then did Dickson realize he had run out of ammunition.

"God fucking damn it!"

The Hummer disappeared around the rear of the Grand Hotel.

Dickson spun around to face Carter. "Why the fuck didn't you take a shot?"

"The bitch stole my guns. Remember?"

Dickson gave him the finger with one hand while he keyed the radio with the other. "They're getting away. Williamson, round up the others and meet me here. Joel, where the fuck are you?"

JOEL ROLLED ONTO his side, consciousness coming back slowly. When he rubbed his forehead he winced, the pain snapping him back to reality. He remembered that Rebecca beat him up for some reason. Jesus, what had gotten into that bitch? When he got his hands on her he'd—

Dickson's voice came over the radio. "*Joel, where the fuck are you?*"

Shit, he'd promised to bring the pick-up around front. Panic washed over him. He rolled onto his other side, relieved to see the Chevy still there. Then he noticed the bed open and that Rebecca, Diana, and the kids were missing. A Hummer raced across the parking lot behind the hotel heading out of the area. Dickson would kick his—

"*Joel, you better answer me right now or I'm going to feed you to the fucking deaders.*"

Joel found the radio and picked it up. He keyed the Talk button as he climbed to his feet. "I'm here, boss. I—"

"I don't care. Bring the pick-up to the front of the building now."

Getting to his feet, Joel headed for the Chevy and stumbled, banging his thigh against the tailgate. After closing the tailgate and cap cover, he climbed into the driver's seat and circled around to the front of the hotel.

WILLIAMSON HEARD THE gunfire from the roof above him,

tires squealing, and Dickson freaking out over the radio. He felt his groin tighten as he fought back the urge to piss himself. It sounded like the entire group was collapsing around him. They had been in tough scrapes before, but nothing this bad. He had seen Dickson go nuts once before on a trucker they found in a rest area who refused to take Dickson's shit. The boss beat the guy nearly to death, set fire to his rig, and left the poor bastard to be eaten by deaders. Now he lost it on his own people. Williamson didn't mind being part of the group as long as they took what they wanted and got some pussy now and then. But a God damn firefight in the middle of an inferno? Fuck that shit.

Starting the van, Williamson left his hidden position behind the Levi's store and sped down the access road to Route 302, throwing the radio out the window.

STRATMAN HAD OPENED the access hatch leading from the roof into the store when he heard the van start up and pull away. He watched, stunned, as the kid raced down the access road, leaving them behind.

Elaine emerged from Banana Republic and attempted to wave down Williamson, with no success. She yelled and cursed at the van. Stratman fired a round into the air, catching her attention. When Elaine looked up at the roof, he raised his radio.

"What happened?" she asked.

"*The little prick abandoned us.*"

"That cocksucker. What happened at the hotel? I heard gunshots."

"*Somehow the targets got away and stole the boss' Hummer. They're heading south toward the other end of the outlet mall. Go that way and see if you can head them off. I'll join you once I get off this roof.*"

"Gotcha. Be careful."

As Elaine turned and headed through the outlet stores,

Stratman climbed down the access hatch into the main store.

NATHAN RACED ACROSS the rear parking lot of the hotel, avoiding the other parked and abandoned vehicles, slowing only when he bumped over the curb onto the grassy segment, not wanting to rip off the transmission.

Alissa spun around in her seat and stared through the shattered rear window. "No one's following us."

"Hopefully, we scared them off."

"Let's get the others and... slow down."

"What's wrong"

"To our right. Two women and two children on the run."

Nathan could not afford to take his eyes off the road. "Are they armed?"

"One has a shotgun. They look in poor shape."

"I suppose you want to go back and get them."

"Of course."

"God damn it," Nathan mumbled under his breath. He slowed and turned the Hummer to the right, closing the range with the group.

One of the women, the least haggard of the group and the one holding the shotgun, placed herself between the Hummer and the others and raised the weapon, though she didn't seem competent with it. Nathan stopped. Alissa opened the door and jumped out, the Mossberg raised and ready to fire.

"Drop your weapon or I'll shoot."

The second woman hugged the children against her.

The first one held her ground. "Are you with Dickson's team?"

"Who the fuck is Dickson?"

"He runs the group."

"If you're talking about the asshole who tried to kidnap us, we almost put a bullet in his head."

The woman lowered her shotgun. "We escaped from him.

I'm Rebecca—"

"Save that for later." Alissa opened the rear door. "Get in."

ELAINE REACHED THE end of the outlet mall and paused to get her bearings. To her left, the couple that had stolen Dickson's Hummer were picking up Rebecca, the bitch, and her kids.

She keyed the radio. "I found them. They're at the end of the outlet mall. They're giving the family and Joel's girlfriend a lift."

DICKSON WATCHED THE Chevy swerve around the rear corner of the hotel and head for them. About fucking time, he thought. The flames had reached the outlet mall. The stores on the opposite side of the access road were already burning and fire had jumped the road and ignited Banana Republic.

The Chevy screeched to a halt in front of him and Joel climbed out. Dickson ran around the front of the vehicle. "Where the fuck were you?"

As Carter limped around back, he peered inside the bed. "They're gone. All three of them."

Dickson grabbed Joel and slammed him against the bed. "Did you let them go? And where is Rebecca?"

Before Joel could answer, Elaine's voice came over the radio.

"I found them. They're at the end of the outlet mall. They're giving the family and Joel's girlfriend a lift."

"Keep an eye on them. We'll be right there."

The glare Dickson gave Joel made the latter piss himself.

"I should shoot you right now."

"Save it for later," Carter climbed into the passenger seat. "Let's get the others first."

Dickson shoved Joel inside the cab and pushed him into the center, then jumped in beside him. He shifted into drive and took off, racing down the road between the outlet mall and the hotel.

CHRIS TOOK A quick glance in his rearview mirror. He noticed two things. First, the fire had closed in behind them, now only two hundred feet to their rear. Second…

"We got company."

Miriam and Kiera spun around.

Off to their right, two hundred deaders staggered toward the gunfire around the hotel. They posed no immediate threat. The danger came from the twenty or so deaders emerging from the trees around the restaurant and filtering in off the street, bearing down on the Ram.

Kiera moved away from the vehicle and approached the nearest deader, which wore a blood-stained National Guard uniform. Its chest and abdomen were riddled with bullet holes and its right arm had been shot off. "I got this."

"No." Miriam tried to stop her.

Kiera neared the Guardsman deader, raised the FAL, and fired a three-round burst. Its head exploded into a shower of blood, bone, and tissue. She didn't pause, stepping around the carcass and moving in on to the next deader, this one wearing a leather greatcoat with its internal organs missing. It snarled as she fired three rounds into its head, blasting it away.

Miriam circled around to Kiera's left, taking out a naked male deader limping toward her daughter. A second strode across the restaurant's entrance dressed in jeans and a plaid wool shirt. A handcuff still hung around its right wrist, the other end holding a chewed off arm. Miriam moved up to it, pumped a round into the chamber, and vaporized its head.

Stepping out from behind the driver's seat, Chris gave a full circle check of the area, making certain he missed no approaching dangers. Once assured nothing would sneak up on them, he used the sniper rifle to pick off those deaders farthest away from

Miriam and Kiera.

In less than two minutes, they had cleared the area. By now, the fire had closed in on them from the front and rear, setting alight everything in the area. Black smoke flowed through the open spaces and ash fell on the parking lot like a soft grey snow.

"Get back in the pick-up," coughed Chris.

The two women joined him. Kiera shook her head, dislodging the ash from her hair. The roar of the inferno could be heard clearly inside the cab.

"We can't stay here much longer," warned Miriam.

"I know." Chris had a nervousness to his voice she had never heard before.

"What should we do?"

Chris raised the radio to his mouth and spoke loud enough to be heard over the fire. "Nathan, we're going to have to move soon. The fire is about to cut us off. Where are you?"

DICKSON CAME AROUND the rear corner of the hotel so fast the rear end of the Chevy fishtailed. He compensated and raced across the parking lot, coming within inches of clipping the front bumper of a Prius.

"Slow down," said Carter. "You're going to get us killed."

"Fuck you. I won't let those bastards—"

"Over there." Joel pointed to the right where the Hummer picked up Rebecca and the others.

Dickson swerved in their direction and floored the Chevy. The engine knocked and pinged in protest. He ignored it, focusing his attention and his fury on the Hummer. The last of the kids climbed in back.

"Send them a message," Dickson ordered.

Carter crinkled his eyebrows. "How?"

"Shoot them."

Carter hesitated. After a moment, he figured hanging out

the window of a speeding vehicle driven by a lunatic was preferable to pissing off Dickson. He reached in back and took an AK-47 off the back seat, rolled down the passenger door window, and climbed out, sitting on the ledge. Holding the inside handlebar with his left hand, he aimed with the right. He bounced around too much to get a good aim.

"Hold my shirt."

"Me?" asked Joel.

"Yeah, asshole. And you better not let go."

As Joel held him in place, Carter raised the semi-automatic and aimed at Alissa.

CONNIE CRAWLED INTO the Hummer last, sitting on her mother's lap. Alissa closed the door and yelled through the window.

"Hang on tight. It's going to get rough in—"

Three gunshots rang out. Two whizzed by her head. The third struck the right rear fender, ricocheted off, and clipped her arm. She looked down to see blood oozing from a three-inch cut across her upper arm. Three more shots rang out, two punching into the Hummer's tailgate and the third missing her head by inches. Connie screamed and hugged her mother.

Diana shifted in her seat. "Oh, shit. It's Dickson."

"We've dealt with him already." Alissa jumped into the front seat." Let's go."

Nathan floored it and pulled away a moment before three more rounds sailed past where the Hummer had been parked. Reaching the ring road around the outlet mall and the hotel, he made his way to Chris and the others.

FROM HER POSITION at the end of the outlet mall, Elaine watched the Hummer speed past, followed a few seconds later by the Chevy. She ran out and waved for Dickson to pick her up. He ignored her and passed by, intent on catching the Hummer.

Elaine broke into a sprint and followed the two vehicles.

RACING THROUGH THE outlet mall, Stratman found himself in a tunnel of fire as the stores on either side of him ignited. Embers fell on his arms and shoulders, searing the skin underneath. He brushed them off before they roasted him alive, which probably would not happen before he suffocated from the thick smoke surrounding him.

He saw a break between the stores up ahead and to the right and ran for it, praying it didn't lead into a dead end. It crossed a courtyard that opened onto a parking lot in the southwest corner of the mall. Stratman ran as fast as he could, stopping only when his lungs gave out. He dropped to his knees, inhaled, and coughed furiously. It felt as if he would hack his lungs out of his chest. Finally, after one intense cough that hurt his chest muscles, he hocked up a wad of black mucus and took in deep breaths. God damn, he might live for another few minutes.

Two vehicles sped past the parking lot, the Hummer in the lead with Dickson in hot pursuit in the Chevy. Carter hung out the passenger window, firing on them. A few seconds later, Elaine ran behind them. Stratman laughed to himself. Maybe he wouldn't live as long as he thought.

Standing up and taking a moment to steady himself, Stratman set off after the others.

"HERE THEY COME." Kiera leaned forward and pointed to the access road from the hotel that ran by the restaurant.

Chris stepped out of the Ram and waved them down. Nathan slowed and pulled alongside him. Chris noticed a pile of people in the back seat.

"Where did you get…?"

"Never mind that." Nathan pointed behind him. "He's our main concern."

As if on cue, the Chevy rounded the corner and bore down on them. Someone sat outside the passenger window, firing an AK-47. The rounds chewed up the pavement around the Hummer and punched into the tailgate. Alissa grabbed Nathan's FAL and stepped out of the vehicle. She fired off the entire magazine, sweeping the barrel back and forth.

One bullet went through the passenger side of the windshield, striking the gunman in the gut, who dropped his AK-47. One punched into the front grill. One ricocheted off the hood, blasting through the window in front of the driver. Another struck the left front tire, blowing it out. The front end of the Chevy swerved from right to left as someone inside the cab tried to hold the wounded gunman in place. The Chevy lurched violently to the right and overturned. When it toppled onto its side, the roof tore the gunman in half, the upper body being flung through the air and landing with a sickening splat ten yards from the Hummer. The Chevy rolled over once, landing on the curb of the dividing island, teetered for a minute, then toppled upright onto its wheels.

"Cool," called out Kiera, ignoring the glare Miriam flashed her.

Alissa smiled at Kiera then turned to Nathan and Chris. "We have to get out of here. This entire place is about to go up in flames."

"You lead," said Nathan.

Jumping into the Ram, Chris exited the restaurant parking lot and turned onto Route 302, heading south.

UPON REACHING ROUTE 302, Williamson found a flaming set of overhead traffic signals collapsed on and blocking the main road, forcing him to navigate through several parking lots to escape, which became more difficult by the minute. Flames engulfed every building on the west side of Route 302, spreading to the abandoned vehicles in the parking lots. He had to turn back onto the main road when he reached the entrance to the Saco River Camping Area, a wooded enclosure that burned fiercer than anything in Conway.

Williamson stopped when he reached the merger between Routes 302 and 16, only half a mile from the Grand Hotel and the outlet mall. He couldn't go any further. The conflagration had passed south of North Conway, followed the forest, and connected with the fire burning its way down the western side of the city, both having converged at this location. Everything around him burned. Fallen, flaming trees blocked Route 16. What remained of North Conway comprised an untouched area of less than a square mile, which the fire would soon consume.

Everyone was trapped inside this area.

Along with several hundred deaders.

Chapter Nineteen

WILLIAMSON STARED AT the inferno blocking his escape. He couldn't go back, not after abandoning the group and making a run for it. Carter might have kicked his ass again to teach him a lesson, but the way Dickson ranted over the radio, Williamson would be lucky if Dickson killed him quickly. He had only one option.

He drove into the firestorm.

Flames from the woods and burning buildings reached out for the van. The outside temperature registered one hundred and twenty-seven degrees. He tried rolling down the windows, but black smoke poured in, making it difficult to breath. The engine thermometer slowly climbed, reaching the red zone. Thankfully, the roads remained clear of debris and other vehicles, allowing him clear sailing. A quarter of a mile ahead of him, Williamson saw open road. He'd made it. In a few minutes he'd be—

A burning pine along the side of the road toppled over, landing on the front hood of the van, caving in the engine compartment and shattering the windshield. Williamson screamed, not from fear or the broken glass that flew into his face, but from the fact the tree crushed the dashboard against his legs. He could still move his feet, so no bones were broken. When he yanked at his legs, they were wedged in place. Leaning forward, he reached for the seat adjustor, hoping to move it back. He had no room for his hand under the caved in dashboard.

The flames from the fallen tree spread into the van, setting the interior on fire.

Fuck.

Williamson punched the dashboard in desperation, which gave him an idea. Placing his palms against the surface, he pushed up, hoping to raise it enough to move his legs. It didn't work. Maybe if he—

The van's side windows burst, allowing the fire to roll in and turn the inside of the van into a furnace, surrounding Williamson. At least the end would be quick.

Williamson guessed wrong.

The clothes seared off his body in seconds. The skin, muscles, and tissues burned more slowly as the intense heat evaporated the water within him. Once his body had dried out, the epidermis caught fire, burning off and peeling away. The blood in his veins and arteries dried out and clotted, clogging his circulatory system. A few seconds later, those same veins and arteries began to melt. Next, the dermis caught fire, shrinking under the heat and bursting open, the fissures leaking fat onto the charred upholstery. The agonizing pain should have killed Williamson a minute ago. Fear and the adrenaline pumping through his body kept him on the brink of death physically, although his mind had long since gone insane. Williamson inhaled. The heated air dried out his mouth and lungs, depriving him of oxygen. He gasped for breath, unable to take in air, thrashing about the cabin in panic. Finally, after more than a minute of agony, Williamson slumped forward and fell against the steering wheel, fire consuming his body.

CHRIS DROVE UNTIL he reached the intersection of Routes 16 and 302 then stopped. Nathan pulled up alongside the Ram and rolled down the window, motioning for him to do the same. When Chris lowered it, a blast of heat raced through the pick-up.

"Why'd you stop?" asked Alissa. He could barely hear her over the roar of the fire.

"Both ways out are blocked."

"Can't we try to make a break?"

"And end up like him?" Chris pointed to the burning van.

"Shit!" Nathan ran his hand over his head. "We're fucked."

"Not necessarily," Alissa replied. "If we can find a large, flat area of concrete we might be able to ride this out."

"You mean like a parking lot?" asked Nathan.

"Exactly. With luck, it'll pass by us."

"With luck?" asked Chris.

"It's either that or be burned alive."

Miriam leaned forward and pointed to their left. "There's a Lowe's and a JC Penny over there. Will they do?"

"Perfect. Follow us." Alissa raised the window as Nathan pulled away, turned left, and headed for what they hoped would be safety.

ELAINE GASPED WHEN she saw that bitch fire at Dickson and the Chevy flip over. She dropped to her knees and vomited when Carter was torn apart and flung aside. By the time she regained her composure, the assholes had climbed into their vehicles and left.

For a moment, she panicked. Williamson had stolen the van and the assholes the Hummer, and now the Chevy had been wrecked. As far as she could tell, the others were dead and she had no means of escape. Fire surrounded her on all sides. She had to make a run for it. She'd either find a way out or a safe place to hole up until the firestorm passed.

Wiping her mouth clean, Elaine stood and ran across the restaurant's parking lot.

STRATMAN FROZE, UNCERTAIN what to do. The fire had all

but enclosed him in a kill zone. The hotel and outlet mall had become a conflagration, every flammable structure on fire. He didn't have enough time to make it to Route 302 before that exit would be blocked off, and the copse of trees to the left were already in flames. He had one chance of survival, as thin as it might be. A driveway cut through the trees to an open area beyond, a two-hundred-foot-dash down a fire tunnel. Stratman had no other options.

Running across the access road, he plunged into the inferno.

DICKSON MOANED AND rolled his head from side to side. He smelled blood and heard a moan. Deaders. He woke with a start, searching for the approaching danger while feeling around for the Colt, relieved to see no immediate threat. At least from deaders. The firestorm drew closer.

He checked the cab. Joel lay across the front seat, resting in a pool of blood, a large bruise on his forehead. At first, Dickson thought the blood came from Joel until he noticed Carter's severed legs on the passenger floor. Joel moaned and rolled onto his side. Figures this prick survived while a good man like Carter died.

Dickson slapped his face. "Wake up, asshole."

"What's going on?"

"Those fuckers got away, again."

"Let them go." Joel sat up and leaned against the door. "We need to get out of here."

"I'm not going to let those bastards get away with this."

"We know where they are. We can take them down later."

"Fuck that." Dickson turned the ignition on the Chevy. The engine started. "Are you in or out?"

"I'm in."

Dickson tore out of the access road and onto Route 302.

NATHAN IGNORED THE zombies they passed to reach the parking lots. The one in front of Lowe's was the largest and, fortunately, had only a handful of vehicles parked in it. By now, everything around the lot, including Lowe's and the adjacent JC Penny, were on fire. Nathan stopped in the center of the lot. Chris parked a few yards behind them.

"So now we wait it out?" asked Nathan.

"Not in the cars," said Alissa. "They're flammable. Besides, the only air fit to breathe is on the ground."

Nathan looked around. Over two hundred deaders approached from the southwest corner of Lowe's and fifty more wandered through the area, each of them attracted by the newcomers. "We'll be a buffet if we go out there."

"We'll be a barbecue if we stay in here." Alissa grabbed her Mossberg and climbed out, then circled around the other side and opened the rear door. "Everyone out and lay on the ground. Stay at least twenty feet from the cars."

"Wh-what about the deaders?" Diana seemed on the brink of losing it.

"We'll take care of them. Hurry."

As Diana ushered the kids out and helped them to the ground, Rebecca stepped over to Alissa and held up the Remington. "Can I get a gun? This thing's almost out of ammo."

"Do you know how to shoot?"

"I'll learn."

Alissa handed her Carter's AK-47. "Thanks."

Chris and the others joined her. "What are we doing?"

"Making a last stand."

"Great," chided Kiera. "We read about Custer in school. That didn't go well."

Alissa pointed to Diana and the kids. "Miriam, do we have any masks for them?"

"I can make some." She placed her Mossberg against the Hummer, took off her sweater and then her shirt, and began tearing the latter into strips.

Nathan and Rebecca had already begun picking off the deaders scattered across the parking lot. Alissa and Chris concentrated on those near Lowe's.

"THERE THEY ARE." Dickson pointed into Lowe's parking lot. "There they are."

He spotted them from Route 302 and veered off, barreling across the JC Penny parking lot toward them, passing by ten deaders. He had the motherfuckers trapped.

"They'll see us," warned Joel.

"They have too much to worry about."

Dickson gunned the engine, heading straight toward Alissa.

MIRIAM HAD FINISHED handing out the make-shift masks when she heard an engine off to the right. The Chevy passed in front of JC Penny and bore down on them.

"Incoming."

Nathen spun around and aimed the FAL, emptying the rest of his magazine into the front grill.

DICKSON DID NOT duck when the rounds smashed into the pick-up. He did swear when every light on the dashboard lit up and the engine gave out. With the last of the Chevy's momentum, he turned left. Opening the door, he dived out and pulled that idiot Joel across the seat to safety as another round of bullets tore into the pick-up.

As Joel lay on the round whimpering, Dickson moved behind the left front wheel for cover, popped up, and fired the AK-47 he took from the back seat into the Hummer, blowing out two tires and sending the others ducking for cover.

Then he spotted that bitch Diana and her two brats

sprawled on the ground. He reloaded and took aim.

As THE AK-47 rounds slammed into the Hummer, Alissa realized the danger Diana and the kids were in. Jumping into the driver's seat, she backed up and swung left, putting the vehicle between them and Dickson as a second round of gunfire pelted the vehicle. The shots were aimed low, most punching into the tires and the lower body. One round ricocheted around the cab, ripping a chunk of flesh from her right forearm. Blood spread across her shirt.

Alissa crawled across the cab and fell out the passenger side, taking cover behind the front tire.

Nathan saw the blood on her arm. "You're hit."

"It's a flesh wound. Miriam, let me have one of those pieces of cloth."

Miriam rushed over, leaving Diana and the kids on the ground.

They did not notice the deader sneaking up behind them, a North Conway police officer still wearing its bullet-proof vest.

Kiera did. She ran out from behind the Ram and aimed at the deader. When she fired the FAL, the rounds blasted away its neck. The deader teetered for a moment, its head wobbling on the exposed spine before dropping off. The body collapsed into a heap, congealed blood oozing from its neck. The head rolled around like a football, coming to rest so it faced Kiera, its mouth snapping at her. Kiera blew the head apart with three more rounds.

The parking lot became a blood sport arena, Alissa and Nathan engaged in a gun battle with Dickson, Miriam and Kiera crouched behind them taking down any deaders that drew close, and Chris behind the Ram clearing away the deaders approaching from Lowe's.

STRATMAN BROKE THROUGH into open air, thanking a God he didn't believe in for letting him live so long. He kept running, wanting to put as much distance between himself and the flames as possible. He finally gasped for breath, inhaled smoke from the fire, and began coughing. Pulling his shirt up around his mouth to filter away the smoke, he ran as fast as he could.

His energy gave out when he reached the far edge of the Lowe's parking lot. Stratman collapsed onto his back. Every time he took in air, he coughed and wheezed. He inhaled deeply and hacked, spitting out black sputum. After that, he caught his breath.

That's when he heard gunfire.

Rolling onto his stomach, he spotted Dickson crouched behind the Chevy battling it out with the others in the center of the lot. A pack of deaders rounded the far end of JC Penny and lumbered toward him, twelve in total. From this vantage point, he could easily take them down before they overran the boss. Stratman aimed the hunting rifle on the closest deader, what used to be a teenage girl with her face chewed off. His finger wrapped around the trigger.

Stratman lowered the rifle.

This was insanity. What had been an attempt to take the cabin from the newcomers became a lust for revenge. He had seen Dickson obsessed before and it never turned out well. He refused to die for this.

Stratman placed the rifle beside him, lay low, and prepared to wait out the final moments.

ELAINE MADE IT as far as the Quality Inn when she ran into a pack of thirteen deaders lumbering toward the sound of battle. Upon spotting Elaine, they surged in her direction. She could only move forward because of the fire surrounding her on all sides, and she would never outfight or outrun that many deaders. To her left, the roof of the Quality Inn already burned. Her only chance lay with going through the motel and circling around the pack, coming out the other side.

Elaine bolted for the entrance.

The glass doors did not slide open due to the lack of electricity. Elaine fired her weapon three times, blowing out the pane, then pushed through into the lobby. No deaders were inside. A sign by the elevators indicated the outdoor pool was to the right. Crossing the lobby, she turned down the corridor.

And stopped short.

Deaders filled the corridor, shambling toward her, attracted by the noise she had made. Spinning around, another pack from the corridor opposite the lobby also closed in.

The stairs to the second floor stood off to her left, with only one deader blocking her path. She blasted it apart with her AK-47, pushed past the body, and ran upstairs. As she turned onto the landing, a young boy deader in a Pokémon t-shirt centered itself at the top of the stairway and snarled. A three-round burst from the weapon blew it against the far wall. Elaine ran up to the second floor.

"Fuck!"

Flames had burned through the ceiling in several places and smoke filled the building. Deaders packed the corridor up here as well, although most were at the far ends, clawing at the windows. Upon hearing the gunshot and seeing Elaine, they lurched down the corridor.

Elaine ran over to the room opposite the stairs and tried the door. It was locked. Something on the other side slammed into it and snarled. She ran down to the next door. It was also locked. Fear overtook her. She tried each door in turn, finding none of them open. With each minute, a horrible death drew nearer. At the fifth door, she found the keycard still in the lock. The nearest deader had closed to within ten feet. Elaine removed the card and reinserted it. The green light flashed. She smelled the decayed breath of the deader as it charged.

Shoving the door open, she pushed her way into the room and slammed shut the door. Several dead hands scratched at the outside.

A hungry growl emanated from behind her.

Elaine spun around to see an obese male deader wearing only boxer shorts lumbering toward her. She ducked as it drew close, passing by the obese deader as it crashed into the door. Circling around the bed, Elaine rushed over to the window, shoved it aside, and punched out the screen. A strip of grass lay beneath her. If she didn't break her leg, she would be fine.

Swinging her right leg out the window, Elaine prepared to jump when the obese deader attacked, pinning her left leg inside the room. Its dead hands clawed at her, scratching her face. Elaine raised her hands to protect herself. The obese deader lowered its hands, ripping open her shirt and tearing its way into her abdomen. Elaine screamed. The pain was unbearable, but not as much as when the deader yanked out a segment of her intestine and shoved it into its mouth. It backed away, releasing the pressure on Elaine's leg. She dropped out the open window, her intestines unwinding as she fell. She landed on her shoulders, snapping her spine.

As Elaine's life flowed from her body, her dying vision was of the obese deader standing by the open window, pulling up her intestines bit by bit to feed.

ALISSA'S MOSSBERG RAN out of ammunition. She went to reload. "Shit."

"What's wrong?" asked Nathan.

"I'm almost out."

Nathan checked his own supply. "I'm down to three magazines."

Alissa turned to Miriam and Kiera. A ring of deader corpses spread out on front of them. "How are you two doing for ammunition?"

"We should have enough to take care of these," answered Miriam.

"But we don't have enough to take out Chris' horde," added Kiera.

Alissa checked out Lowe's. Both it and JC Penny were on fire. Chris had taken down half the horde, but almost one hundred remained. They were at the peak of the crisis. If they survived the next few minutes, they had a good chance of making it out alive. At this moment, though, the odds were stacked against them.

DICKSON HID BEHIND the Chevy to reload. At this rate, he'd run out of ammunition or get shot before this gunfight ended. He needed help, but that prick Joel was of no use. He sat against the door to the Chevy, holding his legs against his chest, his head resting on his knees. Dickson leaned over and slapped him across the head.

"Snap out of it, asshole."

"What?"

"We need to outflank them."

Joel stared, dumbfounded. "How?"

"I'll lay down cover fire. When I do, charge the Hummer and kill them."

"And get cut down out in the open? No fucking way."

Dickson leveled his AK-47 at Joel's head. "Then get shot right here. Your choice."

Joel stared at him, slowly realizing Dickson meant it. Removing the last AK-47 from the rear seat, Joel moved to the end of the Chevy, crouching behind the bed. He checked his weapon and nodded. As Dickson popped up and laid down suppressing fire, Joel ran around the end of the Chevy and charged the Hummer.

"IT CAN'T END this way."

Chris watched the roof of Lowe's cave in, sending dust and flames billowing skyward. The side wall collapsed, crushing a score of deaders. There were still too many, and he had only twenty or so rounds left. Burnt alive, eaten alive, or gunned down by thugs. There had to be another way out.

The front wall of Lowe's steamed from where the internal fire heated it. In the far-right corner, near where the deaders passed, stood the gated area containing the twenty- and forty-pound propane tanks. If they had to go out, at least they would do so with a bang.

"Everyone hit the deck," he yelled across the parking lot.

Chris aimed the sniper rifle at the propane tanks and fired seven rounds into them.

Chapter Twenty

THE INTENSE HEAT surrounding the tanks caused the propane inside to expand, putting pressure on the containers. When the bullets struck, the gas erupted and was ignited by the flames and embers. A massive fireball expanded outward, engulfing the closest deaders. The blast wave bowled over every deader, blew away a large section of wall, and sent shrapnel flying across the parking lot. Of even greater danger were the seven tanks punctured by Chris' bullets. They tore through the area like rockets, destroying everything in their path. One slammed into the passenger door of the Ram, bashing in the side and pushing it sideways several inches. Two ripped through the horde, taking out nearly a dozen of the living dead. Three shot harmlessly across the parking lot.

The last, a forty-pound tank, struck Joel as he rushed the Hummer. It caught him in the chest, pulverizing his ribcage and crushing his upper body, and ripping off the front of his head. The tank traveled another two hundred feet, dragging Joel's corpse most of the way before the body dropped and rolled into a bloody mass on the pavement.

The explosion also blew open the back of JC Penny. With the rapid increase in oxygen, the flames inside the store exploded into a giant fireball. Most of it billowed skyward and burst through the weakened roof, contained by the remaining walls. A wave of fire blasted out the front doors and cascaded across the parking lot, setting alight the twelve deaders out front.

As the shock of the explosion wore off, Miriam crawled over to Diana and the kids. "Are you okay?"

"I think so," said Diana. "Just a little shaken up."

Kiera rolled into a crouching position, waved to her mother, and scanned the area. The deaders had all been knocked off their feet. Most were attempting to stand. Kiera picked them off one by one.

Rebecca had seen Joel running toward them a moment before the explosion. When she raised her head, she no longer saw him, only a heap of shattered tissue wearing his clothes that lay on the other side of the parking lot. She felt no remorse, no sadness, nothing but a sense that Joel got what he had deserved.

"Check on Chris," said Nathan. "I'll keep the Chevy covered."

Alissa stayed low and rushed over to the Ram, circling around back. She found Chris lifting himself onto his elbows, shaking his head.

"Serves you right, dumb ass. What were you thinking?"

"I was trying to save our lives." He pointed toward Lowe's. "I think I did a pretty good job."

Alissa glanced in the direction of the horde. "You've got to be fucking kidding."

Chris followed her gaze. Twenty deaders had gotten to the feet and stumbled toward them, their bodies burning.

DICKSON WAITED UNTIL the debris stopped falling. His ears still rang from the blast. He raised his head slowly, brought his weapon to bear, and scanned the area between him and the Hummer, fearing the others might be charging. Nothing except the mangled body of Joel, who had been caught in the blast. No fucking loss.

Moaning caught his attention. He spun around. Two deaders, one in a yellow road worker's vest and hardhat, the other a woman with both hands torn off above the wrists, both in flames, were less than a few yards away. Dickson fired at the deader in the vest. The round reflected off the hardhat. He steadied his aim and fired again, this time catching the deader in the mouth and blowing out the back of its head. Dickson switched targets and fired. The weapon clicked.

Fuck.

As he reloaded, the handless deader attacked, its stumps vainly grabbing for something to hold on to. Ten more deaders were behind it. Dickson shoved the handless deader back into the closest one, causing them both to fall over. He finished reloading, crouched by the Chevy, and took out the two deaders, his attention drawn away from the shooters.

NATHAN SAW THE battle play out between Dickson and the deaders, which gave him an idea.

"Alissa?"

She appeared from behind the Ram and Nathan waved for her to join him. Alissa crouched and rushed over.

"What's up?"

"Dickson is pre-occupied with the deaders. We have a chance of taking him out."

"How?"

Nathan pointed to the JC Penny building. "I'll provide cover while you and Rebecca head for the corner. Once you two are in place, lay down cover fire and I'll charge him. Try to conserve ammo since we're low."

Alissa shifted her position to Rebecca. "Are you up to this?"

"If it means we take out that son of a bitch, yes."

Alissa nodded to Nathan. "Let's do this."

Nathan raised his hand and flipped it, extending one finger. He did it again with a second finger, and the last time with three. Alissa and Rebecca ran around the rear of the Hummer and toward JC Penny as Nathan stood, protected by the hood, and pumped a single round every two seconds into the Chevy, stopping only when the woman reached their spot. He still had some rounds left in the magazine but switched it out with a full one. When finished, he waved to Alissa. She waved back and began the countdown with her fingers.

ONLY A HANDFUL of deaders remained. Dickson had enough ammunition to deal with them and show those assholes a thing or two. This was far from—

Gunfire tore into the Chevy from the direction of the Hummer, punching through the metal around the engine. Who did those motherfuckers think they were? He would take a lot of pleasure in watching them suffer.

When the shooting stopped, Dickson counted to three and stood. Sure enough, that dick who had tried to kill him earlier in the office had rounded the rear of the Hummer and charged.

Dickson raised his AK-47.

REBECCA MOVED AWAY from the corner of the building, crouched, and raised her AK-47 as Dickson stood and lowered his against Nathan. She fired through the cab, hoping to be the one who killed the bastard. The frame scattered most of the bullets. By the way he screamed and flinched, some must have struck home.

Alissa dodged to the rear of the Chevy, crouched behind the bed, and leaned around the fender, aiming at Dickson. He spotted her and fired a split second before she did. The bullets missed. She ducked behind the truck, her round firing harmlessly into the air.

Rebecca circled around the front of the Chevy, blasting away at the hood. None of the shots struck home.

Dickson fell back into the blazing zombies.

Alissa and Rebecca met by the driver's side of the Chevy. Rebecca raised her weapon and centered it on Dickson's back. Alissa placed her hand on the barrel and lowered it.

"Why did you do that? I could have killed him."

Alissa nodded toward Dickson. "He doesn't deserve to go peacefully."

THOSE ASSHOLES WERE closing in on him from three sides. Dickson knew if he didn't move now, he'd be fucked. There were only ten of the living dead between him and safety. He would get out of the area, wait for the firestorm to pass, then come back and kill these motherfuckers one at a time.

His chances of survival would have been good if he had circled around the left of the pack. Instead, he charged into them, determined to fight his way out.

The closest three deaders were easy targets. He shot a fourth in its face, blasting it over backwards. Spinning around to the fifth, a male in a blood-covered sweater, he shoved the barrel against its mouth and pulled the trigger.

Nothing happened.

The deader clutched Dickson by the shirt. He felt the fire from its charred hands searing his face as it pulled him in to feed. Dickson raised his arms, breaking its grip, then battered the stock of his AK-47 into its face three times. It staggered backwards and fell over. Dickson patted out the flames that had sprung up on his shirt, burning the skin beneath.

A snarl from behind caught his attention. A deader that had once been a child no more than ten, and whose face had been chewed off, snuck up on him. Dickson swung around, crashing the stock of his AK-47 into its head with such force that he snapped its neck. He raised a foot and kicked out, sending the thing sprawling.

Turning around, he watched as two deaders collapsed, their muscles having been burned away, rendering them immobile. They fell to the pavement, still clutching at him with withering arms.

Dickson kicked one in the face, laughing. "You can't beat me, you motherfucking deaders. I'm better than all of you bast—"

The last two deaders, one a female in a tattered, gore-stained nurse's uniform and the other a man wearing a blood-soaked Red Cross armband, lunged forward as their legs gave out. Both tumbled into Dickson, pushing him over. He fell so hard it knocked the breath out of him. Those few seconds of disorientation sealed his fate. The two deaders pulled themselves onto Dickson. Their clothes set his own on fire. The agonizing pain as the flesh seared from his body snapped him back to full consciousness. The Red Cross deader had burned to the point it could no longer function. It fell to the side, landing on Dickson's legs, pinning them. Grabbing the Red Cross deader by the back of its hair, Dickson yanked, succeeding only in tearing out a clump of hair from its decayed flesh. It clawed at his abdomen, tearing open his shirt and digging into flesh. The nurse deader reached in, wrapped its hands around his organs, and yanked them out, stuffing his lungs into its mouth.

Dickson felt none of this. His shirt had already melted into his skin. Like a slab of meat, the outer skin charred while the tissues and muscles cooked. The flames reached his face, drying up his eyes until they collapsed and charred the inside of his mouth. Fortunately for Dickson, his agony only lasted thirty seconds before his corpse combined in a funeral pyre with the two deaders that had eviscerated him.

ALISSA DID NOT feel the satisfaction she thought she would watching Dickson die. Not that she mourned his death. She didn't. His demise served as another reminder of the constant violence that dominated this new world.

The firestorm reached its apex. Everything surrounding the parking lot burned, including the two commercial buildings. She could feel the heat against her exposed skin. A strong wind raced across the open area as the conflagration, desperate to stay alive, sucked in all available oxygen.

Alissa tapped Rebecca's shoulder. "We gotta move."

The two women ran to the other side of the Chevy, telling Nathan to follow. They raced back to the Hummer. The others already lay face down, Chris in between Miriam and Kiera near the Ram, and Diana and her kids between the two vehicles, her arms wrapped around their shoulders. Alissa scanned the area for any remaining deaders and, seeing none, crawled onto the ground.

The roar reminded her of the old furnace in the basement of her grandmother's house, only now intensified a hundred times. She had never experienced heat so intense in her life. As the wind increased, she found it increasingly difficult to breathe and gasped for air.

Alissa's last thought before her vision closed in was, "After all I've been through, please don't let me die this way."

Chapter Twenty-One

SOMETHING STIRRED ALISSA. At first, she had no idea what, then it happened again. Someone gently shook her shoulder. This time accompanied by a voice.

"Wake up."

Alissa rolled over and opened her eyes, half expecting to find herself in the afterlife. Kiera and Nathan knelt beside her, with the others watching from a distance, all except Chris who kept his back to the group, scanning the parking lot for danger.

"I'm glad you're all right." Kiera smiled and hugged Alissa. "We were worried about you."

"How long have I been out?"

"Over an hour," said Nathan.

"What happened?"

"The firestorm burnt itself out. It's heading south."

Alissa sat up and looked around. Everything around them had been consumed, leaving behind the charred remains of trees and buildings, along with smaller fires scattered throughout the area. She spotted the inferno to their south, a deadly wall pushing its way across the countryside.

Alissa got to her feet. When she stood, her head spun. Nathan grabbed her before she fell.

"Thanks," she smiled, spending more time in his arms than she needed to.

"You're welcome." He steadied Alissa. "Are you ready to head home?"

"How are we getting there?"

"The Ram is banged up pretty bad thanks to Chris—"

Chris turned to the group. "You're welcome for saving your lives."

"—but will still get us home. Everything else is shot up too bad to drive."

"It'll be cozy," added Kiera.

Everyone climbed into the Ram. Nathan drove and Chris road shotgun, with Alissa in between them. Diana, Connie, and Brian sat in the back seat. Rebecca and Miriam rode in the rear, with Kiera providing cover. Nathan left the parking lot, turned north onto Route 302, and headed home.

STRATMAN PLAYED DEAD for almost two hours, lying in the parking lot and hoping no one would notice him. After what those crazy bitches did to Dickson, he didn't want to be next on the revenge list.

After the Ram drove off, Stratman waited a few minutes before getting up. He checked out the Hummer and Chevy, but both were shot up too bad to be going anywhere. Of the few other vehicles in the parking lot, none were usable. That left only one option.

Slinging his hunting rifle over his shoulder, Stratman made his way to the main road and walked north.

A BUZZ OF excitement raced through the cabin upon their return. Steve and Little Stevie were glad to see everyone made it back alive and stunned to see their ranks had grown. Shithead was the happiest of all, thoroughly sniffing the newcomers before begging for attention. Archer sat by the patio doors for a few minutes before disdainfully going upstairs.

Once the introductions had been made, Alissa tended to

everyone's wounds, starting with the newcomers. Rebecca was fine except for some physical trauma she had experienced the first day with Dickson's group, which had been healing well. The same could not be said for Diana and her kids. Except for Brian's broken arm, which she would reset later, there were no major physical injuries. However, being held captive for so long in such poor conditions had taken its toll. All three suffered from malnutrition and dehydration as well as sores from being filthy for so long. These were all reversible with time. The emotional and psychological scars would never go away.

As Miriam took the newcomers upstairs to get them hot showers and new clothes, and as Steve prepared a hot meal, Alissa examined the others. They all came through with nothing worse than a few minor cuts and scrapes. Halfway through the exams, her mind began to focus on the next priority—a possible evacuation.

With the firestorm now south of their location, nothing stood between it and the cabin. A change in wind direction, like what brought the fire into North Conway, could just as easily send it toward them. They would have to load supplies, find another vehicle, and plan an evacuation.

Nathan came over to help Alissa dress the wounds to her arms, following her instructions on how to clean and dress them properly. As he stitched up the chunk taken out of her upper arm, Alissa spoke softly so none of the others would hear.

"Sorry for nearly getting us killed."

"You didn't." Nathan almost sounded like he meant it.

"Yes, I did. I should have listened to you. You didn't trust them. That's why you gave Nora an empty revolver."

Nathan grinned. "I'm a cop. I'm used to seeing the bad side of people."

"I need to let go of my faith in people."

"That's the last thing you want to do."

His answer caught Alissa by surprise. She jerked her head up.

"Keep your arm still. I'm having a tough enough time with this as it is."

"What did you mean by that?" she asked.

"By what?"

"That I need to keep my faith."

"You do." Nathan paused to make eye contact. "I never would have gone in there and risked my life. I would have detained and interrogated Nora, and then let them come to me. If we had done it my way, Rebecca, Diana, and the kids would still be abused by Dickson and the others, or worse. They're alive because of you."

"I know." Alissa sighed. "Still, I need to be less trusting."

Nathan went back to stitching the wound. "You will. That'll come with experience. Don't let it negatively cloud your judgment. If the world ever hopes to survive this nightmare, we're going to need people who hold on to their humanity."

"Thanks."

Nathan finished a few minutes later. As he wrapped the wound in gauze, a low rumble sounded in the distance. Shithead's ears went up. The sound occurred again, this time closer and louder. Shithead whimpered and curled up at Chris' feet. A few seconds later, something struck the roof and deck.

"Oh my God," said Kiera. "It's raining."

They all rushed onto the deck. Rain was an understatement. The area experienced a downpour.

"It's a miracle," mumbled Nathan.

Chris shook his head. "I'm not religious, but you're right."

"How so?" asked Kiera.

"If this lasts long enough, it'll put out that fire."

Kiera's eyes widened. "I never thought of that."

"You don't have to any longer," said Alissa. "We're safe now."

For a while, she added mentally as an afterthought.

Chapter Twenty-Two

STRATMAN MADE HIS way through the woods. Honest to God, green, plush woods. Not that forest of burnt death he had traveled through after leaving North Conway.

He had wanted to get as far away as possible from those assholes who had killed off the rest of his group and from the deaders, both of which he had more than his fill of. He hoped to eventually find another band of survivors he could either tag along with or take control of, or at least a well-stocked cabin he could hole up in for a bit as he planned his next move. Right now, he needed to survive. It had taken him almost a day to reach the spot where the fire had started. After that, he found fresh water to drink and a decent place to get some rest. And he didn't have hordes of deaders to contend with.

Sooner or later someone would stumble across him.

FROM ITS PERCH on top of a nearby ridge, the deader in the weathered and blood-stained hunter's camouflage suit watched the lone human trudge his way through its territory. The other five deaders around it began to groan. It held up its hand. The others went silent. It carefully watched the human. The human was still too far away. Any attempt now to trap him ran the risk of their prey getting away. It bided its time, waiting for the right moment.

After several minutes, the human neared the ridge.

The hunter deader turned to the deader to its side and

grunted. The deader, which wore the soiled remnants of a National Guard uniform, nodded and moaned, loud and prolonged, almost like that of an animal. Another moan echoed from the distance.

They six deaders stood on top of the ridge and waited.

STRATMAN HEARD THE first moan and nearly shit himself. It sounded part deader and part animal. Could animals be turned by those things? The last thing he needed to deal with was a living dead bear or coyote.

A second moan emanated much closer and to his rear, followed a few seconds later by the sound of something, or more appropriately several things, moving through the woods. He had no idea what chased him and did not want to find out.

Stratman ran.

Up ahead he spotted two ridges, a large one and a smaller one that formed a valley. No way would he go in there and get trapped. Stratman turned left to go around them.

THE LEAD DEADER raised its hand, held it for a moment, and dropped it. The deader at the end of the line, the one dressed in a motorcyclist's leather pants and jacket, moaned loudly, its cry distinct from the previous one.

OFF TO STRATMAN'S left, more snarling echoed from the woods. A pack of ten deaders broke through the brush, spreading out to prevent him from passing. Behind him, the other pack emerged, eleven in total.

Fuck. They had him surrounded.

Both packs paused, their milky yet hungry eyes centered on him.

Stratman searched for a way out. He spotted a gap between

the packs several yards wide. If he ran, he might—

The deaders at the end of the two packs spread out, filling the gap.

Stratman shivered as the realization of what happened struck him. He inched his way toward the deaders. They surged forward, their steps careful and precise. They were herding him into the valley.

With no other options open, other than a desperate last stand, he entered the valley.

THE LEAD DEADER nodded its head and groaned. Stepping away, it proceeded to the path descending into the valley. The other five fell in behind it.

STRATMAN MADE IT half-way down the valley. He turned a bend to find another ten deaders blocking his path. They moaned when they saw him but did not move.

A rocky path along the right leading to the top of the ridge provided the only way out. He had enough ammunition to clear a path if—

As if reading his thoughts, the pack moved forward, forcing Stratman to retreat. When he did, they stopped.

A moan came from behind him. The other two packs had entered the valley. They stopped upon catching sight of him and stood still, as if waiting.

Stratman raised his hunting rifle. A deader in a National Guard uniform with a huge chunk of flesh torn from its neck stepped forward three paces and paused. It snarled once, pointed toward Stratman's rifle, and motioned for him to drop it. Stratman could not believe it. Had that thing told him to discard his weapon? When he didn't comply, all three packs became agitated. Stratman held his rifle to the side, crouched, and placed it on the ground. The agitation stopped and the

National Guard deader moved back into line.

The silence ended a minute later. A chorus of moans rose from the three packs. Every deader lowered its head. Stratman turned to the path. Six deaders descended it. As the first one drew near, the pack blocking the path stepped aside, letting it pass. It wore work boots and hunter's camouflage gear, and a plaid shirt stained with dried blood from a wound in its neck. A large gash, more than likely caused by a machete, ran from its upper right forehead, across its nose and mouth, and ending on the right side of the chin.

THE LEAD DEADER approached the human. It smelled fear and resignation. Good. Resignation meant the human would not resist. Fear meant the meat would taste that much better.

Stopping in front of the human, it cocked its head to the side to examine him. The human trembled. It's gaze met the human's, looking deep into his eyes. The human went white and lowered his head.

"Please don't kill me."

The deader recognized the words but had long since forgotten their meaning. It stared at the human a moment then attacked.

Its teeth dug into the human's neck, puncturing deep into its skin. Warm blood squirted into its mouth, moistening its tongue and throat, and quenching a thirst it didn't even realize it had. The deader pulled its head back, tearing off a chunk of flesh. It ate, satisfying its insatiable hunger. It held the human in place as it chewed and swallowed, then took another bite. It would take its fill and then allow the others to feed, making sure the packs each partook of the meal.

It was the proper way.

It was as the Alpha had ordered.

A Preview of
Nurse Alissa vs. the Zombies IV: Hunters

"CAN WE TAKE a break?" Sheri leaned against a tree. She slipped off the Red Sox baseball cap and ran her palm across her forehead, wiping away the sweat. "We've been walking for hours."

"Nut up," replied David. "It's only been ninety minutes since our last break."

"That's still a long time."

Tina grunted in frustration. "Why did we have to bring the prom queen along?"

"Because nobody gets left behind." Brad snapped, quickly ending the argument. The three had been at each other's throats for weeks. If they kept bickering, he might throw himself into a pack of deaders so he wouldn't have to listen to them. It would be quicker and less painful. "Take five."

David and Tina groaned, quieting down when John flashed them an angry glare. They wandered off to get away from the group for a few minutes. Sheri mouthed "Thank you." She slid down the tree into a crouch, opened a bottle of water, and took a long drink. Brad strolled over to a fallen tree, sat down, and sighed. He didn't know how much more of this he could take.

The group had been together since the outbreak began. They were students at Endicott College just north of Salem, Massachusetts. Everyone else on campus were locals and left to be with their loved ones. Brad and several other students from out of state knew they'd never make it home, so they opted to shelter in place. How long could the unrest last? Between the food in their dorms and what they had scavenged from the cafeteria, they had enough supplies to last for weeks. It would not be enough. As the realization dawned on them they were not dealing with rioters but the living dead, the group moved to the second floor of their dorm, filled the stairwells with furniture to prevent the deaders from reaching them, and hunkered down to wait it out.

At that time, there were twenty-nine of them.

They had holed up for two weeks before the deaders occupying the campus stumbled across them by accident. The next five weeks devolved into a siege that ended when a freshman named Randy cracked under the pressure and cleared out a stairwell trying to escape, inadvertently letting the deaders in. The dorm became a slaughterhouse. Only eleven students escaped and headed north.

For some reason, the survivors had turned to Brad for leadership, probably because he was the only senior classman among them. He led the survivors to what hopefully would be the relatively safety of Canada which, at the time, seemed the best option. Three and a half years of college had not prepared him for what they would face out here, and experience came at a high cost. By the time he had figured out how to avoid a deader horde and survive an attack, too many of his group had become casualties. Of those who set out from Endicott, four had been killed by deaders, one died from the elements, and one had taken her own life to spare herself from this nightmare. Their deaths had taught Brad to avoid main roads and travel through the woods. The going had been slow, but it kept them safe. It also kept them cold, tired, and hungry.

John came over and sat beside Brad, taking Brad's hand in his own and squeezing gently. "You okay?"

"Yes," Brad lied. Then he thought better of it. "Not really. I don't know how much longer I can go on."

John chuckled.

"What's so funny?"

"You've said that every week for the past two months, then you pick yourself up and keep going. None of us would have made it this far without you."

"Tell that to Jesse, Sandy, Kevin, and the others."

"They lasted as long as they did because of you. It's not your fault they're dead. This brave, new, fucked up world killed them."

"That's easy for you—"

John placed two fingers on Brad's lips. "You've done a great job. None of us would be following you if we didn't trust you."

Brad winked. "You'd still be here, I hope."

"I would, but I'm biased." John leaned in and kissed Brad. "Time to move out."

They joined Sheri.

"Break time's over," said Brad.

Sheri groaned. She placed the Red Sox cap back on her head, pulling her ponytail through the opening over the back straps.

"Where's Tina and David?" asked John.

Sheri shrugged as she stood, then pointed to an area where the woods were less dense. "They headed in that direction. I assumed they were looking for a place to fuck."

"Shit," mumbled Brad.

John tried to lighten the mood. "At least they've got down the repopulate the world part."

Tina emerged from the woods and whistled. Once she caught their attention, she motioned for them to follow, which they did. When they caught up with her, Brad asked, "Is there a problem?"

"Everything's fine."

"Where's David?"

"There." Tina pointed in front of them.

A field of one hundred square acres stretched before them, two-thirds of it having been enclosed by a wooden fence. A stable sat inside the fence on the opposite side of the enclosure and, just beyond it, a farmhouse. A dozen horses grazed in the center of the corral, ignoring the seven deaders following them along the exterior of the fence, their clutching hands futilely reaching out for the food.

"What's going on?" asked John.

"As far as I can tell," answered David, "those deaders stumbled across the corral and tried to feed off the horses. The farmer went to stop them and was turned."

"Why do you think that?"

"The horses are in great shape. They're well fed and hydrated, which means someone has been taking care of them until recently." David gestured toward a freshly reanimated deader in the center of the pack. "More than likely it was him."

"So?" Sheri asked in a snarky tone. "How does this involve us?"

"Those horses mean we don't have to walk anymore."

"Oh?" Sheri suddenly showed interest.

Brad faced her and grinned. "Now we ride in style."

"Once we get rid of those things," said David, referring to the deaders.

"Let's do this." John led the way to the fence.

Tina whistled to catch the attention of the living dead. They turned as one toward the new source of food. Six of them moaned and staggered in their direction. The farmer, only recently having been turned, snarled and rushed toward them, closing the distance rapidly.

"I got this," said Brad as he positioned himself in front of Tina. He brandished the baseball bat he carried. Tina stayed to his rear, ready to help if necessary.

Brad waited until the deader had come closer and timed his strike carefully. Once within range, he swung the bat, his upper body turning into the blow. It connected with the farmer's head, caving in the left side of its skull. The farmer spun to the right and stumbled but did not go down. As it turned to face

150

him, Brad swung the bat again, this time connecting with the deader's neck. It collapsed into the grass and spasmed. Tina stepped up, positioned the three-foot-long crowbar above its head, and plunged the straight claw through its left eye, churning the metal around to scramble its brain. The deader's body went limp.

Sheri walked up and crossed herself. "Peace be with you. Go with God."

The rest moved on to confront the other deaders, spreading out in a line abreast to present scattered targets. Weeks of experience came in handy. Brad struck down two more with his bat. Tina drove the crowbar through the eye of a third, again churning it around until it collapsed. John lifted his axe and brought it down through the head of the fourth, cleaving it open until the blade reached its jaw. David swung his machete like a bat, severing the head of the fifth from its neck. Sheri moved in against the last deader, a teenage woman in a soiled high school t-shirt. Clutching the right side of its collar in her gloved hand, she drove her bowie knife into the left side of its neck, puncturing the brain stem and twisting. The deader slid off the blade into the grass. As the others approached the corral, Sheri stayed behind to give the same last rights to each corpse as she had done with the farmer.

The horses eyed the newcomers warily. One of them, a tan American Trotter, cautiously made its way over to the fence, sensing these people posed no threat. Tina held out her hand. The horse drew closer, sniffing her palm. Tina placed her hand on the side of its nose and gently rubbed.

"You're a friendly, girl."

The horse playfully nibbled at her hand.

Thirty minutes later, they had settled in the farmer's house after searching it for deaders or survivors, finding none. John returned from checking the stable.

"There are four more horses inside. They're a bit skittish but healthy."

"What about saddles?" asked David.

"There's one for each horse, so we won't have to ride bare-back."

"God be praised," Sheri replied.

"Then it's settled," said Brad. "We'll stay here for the night. Tomorrow we'll take five of the horses and head out."

"What about the others?" asked Tina.

"We'll give them all the hay we can find and leave the corral gate open. That way they'll have a fighting chance."

"Thank you."

David came down from upstairs. "There are two bedrooms up there. One has a king size bed, the other a double."

"Excellent. The girls can share the bigger bed and you can take the double. John and I will take the sofa and recliner."

"I hope this place has hot water," said Sheri. "I could use a nice shower."

"We all could," added Tina.

Brad turned to John, "Check out the kitchen for food. Hopefully. there's something for a good meal. I'll make sure the doors are secured."

Everyone set off about their business, looking forward to the first comfortable night since leaving Endicott.

A Thank You to My Readers

I've been writing short stories as far back as I can remember, but it was Darren McGavin as *The Night Stalker*'s Carl Kolchak that inspired me to be become a writer. It's been one of the most fulfilling things I've done with my life. The best part is having people who read my books and enjoy them. I'm extremely fortunate and grateful that I have a fanbase that devours my novels like zombies eating human flesh. You keep reading and I'll keep writing.

If you liked *Nurse Alissa vs. the Zombies III: Firestorm*, please post a review on Amazon. It doesn't have to be long—just a rating and a sentence or two about why you enjoyed it. The more reviews the *Nurse Alissa vs. the Zombies* series receives, the more opportunity other readers have of discovering the book.

The *Nurse Alissa* saga will continue. The next three books in the series are in various stages of production with at least two more releases planned for 2020.

A second series, which is post-apocalyptic but without zombies, is in pre-production (i.e. I'm researching and plotting out the concept). And my full-length novel *OSS: Office of Supernatural Services*, about Allied intelligence battling Nazi occultism during World War II, is back on track and should be released in early 2021.

Acknowledgments

Writing is solitary and lonely. Getting a book published, on the other hand, is a complicated process involving many people, all of whom deserve to be recognized.

A major thanks goes out to my beta readers: Tammy Michelle Mayberry, Michael Atkinson, Pammy Troupe, Tom Williamson, Marla Dewitt, Dan Uebel, Norma Seitz, Roseann Powell, Doc Fried, Paul Semke, and Cari Laffrenier Thompson. I owe a huge debt of gratitude to Lisa Holland Mastandrea who reviewed the final draft before publication and caught those damnable spelling/grammar errors that always remain hidden during the editing and revision stages.

Christian Bentulan designed the cover art for *Nurse Alissa vs. the Zombies III: Firestorm* as well as the other books in the saga. I love Christian's work. His covers reach out and grab the reader's attention as well as foreshadow what is to come within the pages. Plus, Archer appears on each cover, which he appreciates.

You would not be reading this book, or any of the other in the *Nurse Alissa* series, were it not for my dear friend and colleague Alina Giuchici. I hadn't written a zombie series since *Rotter Apocalypse* was published in 2015. Alina is a major fan of my stories and kept urging me to go back to writing about the living dead. With some gentle shoving in the right direction and a few well-placed ideas, over the course of a long week on the road I came up with the concept of the Alissa series. If you like these books, be sure to thank Alina.

Finally, a major debt of thanks goes to my family, human

and furry. As with my previous novel, I wrote, edited, and released this one during the COVID-19 lockdown because I had so much time on my hands. Being home all the time had its downsides. This has been the best two months of the dogs' lives because they think I quit my job and stayed home all day to be with them, and they want to spend every minute with me. The cats, on the other hand, are more pissed off that I'm around all the time, especially Archer whose naps are disturbed by my typing. (Yes, Alissa's Archer is taken directly from my own cat Archer, especially his asshattery.) It's hard to maintain my writing discipline when everyone is home, but I couldn't do this without their love and support.

About the Author

Scott M. Baker was born and raised in Everett, Massachusetts and spent twenty-three years in northern Virginia working for the Central Intelligence Agency. Scott is now retired and lives just outside of Concord, New Hampshire with his wife and fellow writer Alison Beightol, stepdaughter, two rambunctious boxers, and two cats who treat him as their human servant. He has written *Nurse Alissa vs. the Zombies* and *Nurse Alissa vs. the Zombies II: Escape*, the first two books in his latest zombie apocalypse series; *Shattered World I: Paris*, *Shattered World II: Russia*, and *Shattered World III: China*, the first books in his five-book young adult post-apocalypse series about a group of adventurers attempting to close portals into Hell; *The Vampire Hunters* trilogy, about humans fighting the undead in Washington D.C.; *Rotter World*, *Rotter Nation*, and *Rotter Apocalypse*, his post-apocalyptic zombie saga; *Yeitso*, his homage to the giant monster movies of the 1950s that he loved watching as a kid; as well as several zombie-themed novellas and anthologies.

Please check out Scott's social media accounts for the latest information on future books, upcoming events, and other fun stuff.

Blog: scottmbakerauthor.blogspot.com
Facebook: facebook.com/groups/397749347486177
Twitter: twitter.com/vampire_hunters
Instagram: instagram.com/scottmbakerwriter